OUCH!
tHat 'Hearts'..

OUCH!
tHat 'Hearts'..

Harsh Snehanshu

Srishti
PUBLISHERS & DISTRIBUTORS

SRISHTI PUBLISHERS & DISTRIBUTORS
N-16, C. R. Park
New Delhi 110 019
srishtipublishers@gmail.com

First published by Srishti Publishers & Distributors in 2011
Copyright © Harsh Snehanshu, 2011

Typeset in AGaramond 11pt. by Suresh Kumar Sharma at Srishti

Dedicated to your smile, for being my inspiration to write.

Acknowledgments

Whenever I used to watch any award show on television, I had this feeling that why the hell did the winners thank others when it was the result of their own hard-work and passion? I carried this arrogant feeling until I, myself, achieved something i.e. JEE. When success came, gratitude erupted. I wanted to thank each and everybody who had played a role in this journey, which had just started. I was so euphoric that I even thanked my maid, my primary school friends, the random kids whom I had once played football with and the autowala who used to drop me to school.

In my first book, I'd thanked all those who had been involved, even unknowingly, in making a writer out of me, in shaping my life in ways more subtle than they could imagine. In the second book, I would like to thank some very special people who had been there with me throughout the tough journey of writing the book. I call the journey tough because it required a lot of motivation and patience, and had it not been the support from these special people, the thought of the second book would have remained a thought, rather than a reality.

My first and foremost thanks would go to my father, for being my biggest inspiration. My second token of gratitude goes to my lovely mother, for being cool, progressive and unconditionally supportive, in every endeavour of mine. You're the reason for giving my name its meaning.

Next is my kid sister Saumya for doing all those things which little sisters do to irritate big brothers and still being absolutely adorable.

She is probably going to edit it away but I still want to thank my crazy friend Supriya, simply, for absent mindedly straying into my life and turning it upside down with her humour, wit and sarcasm and never letting my head get too big for my shoulders.

Special thanks to my friend, Akansha Gupta, for being a friend worth treasuring and for being an artist par excellence. The inimitable cover design has been the best 'gift' any artist could ever give to me. Yes, she forgot to charge me a fee.

The acknowledgement wouldn't be complete if I don't thank my reader, Arpa Ray, who came up with this spunky title for the book. Thank you for your persistence.

Lastly, I thank all my readers, writer-friends and critics, some of whom I'd missed last time, especially Shruti Vajpayee, Mitusha, Surabhi, Shirshendu, Giribala aunty, Anirudh, Ankita, Ameen, Jitendra, Ronita, Abhilasha, Sugandha, Tanay and many more for helping me learn and evolve as a writer.

Ah! Finally, I'm done with the sentimental acknowledgements. Now, I can take you to the roller coaster ride of Kanav-Tanya...and OUCH!

Prologue

(From Oops! 'I' fell in love!)

29th August, 2008.

12:45 am. I signed into my Orkut account with my id - *kanav.bajaj* and password -*alldayidreamabouttanya* just to notice that there was an increment in my scraps by almost a century.

Scrolling down the scrapbook, all I could see was my miserly friends wishing me *'Happy Birthday'* in a seemingly festive mood. Their fakeness was obvious as some of them wrote - '*I want a treat*'. They did not even bother to call me to wish and now they were demanding a treat. Extremely pissed off, I didn't even reply a *'Thank you'* to any of them.

Nevertheless, in order to prioritize my acquaintances in a hierarchical order, I flipped through the pages of the scrapbook to get to know who amongst them was the first person to wish me a 'Happy Birthday'.

Interestingly, the first scrap was from an unknown person with no profile picture and '.....'as its name. It said - *'Happy Birthday. May God give you everything you wish for.'*

Bursting with curiosity, I instantly clicked on the profile link. The slow internet speed of my hostel took its own time to open the webpage and played with my curiosity like hell. The profile opened after taking two long painstaking minutes and this was what I saw as the *about me* -

> "I look up at the velvety blackness of the sky
> And I see stars adorning nights dress so bright
> Even diamonds may feel shy

And then I see one
That breaks free and shoots to
I know not where
Oh little star!
Will you take my wish to him who is so far
Tell him that I am
Just a little lonely here...

Hi jerk,
Wanna play Scrabble?"

P.S. This was just the beginning...

Every love story has an end. But this was not true in my case. My story had a beginning in the end and here is where my story really begins.

1. The Beginning

"Hi jerk,
Wanna play Scrabble?"

Ⅰt had been ten minutes and my eyes could not move ahead of the last two lines of her 'about me'. The last two lines did not contain anything about her, neither did they have any great sentiments attached to them but they contained everything about us. I am not talking about me being a jerk (which I am) or the unforgettable scrabble game that it hinted at, but the fact that she was back in my life, exuberantly, was what glued my eyes to the screen. Of course, I wanted to play scrabble! A thousand times. And I could die to hear that word – 'Jerk', one more time.

My tongue was parched except for the saline taste of my tears that somehow managed to creep into my mouth while I was gaping at the dead screen and my body, shivering occasionally, was letting me know that I was still alive.

Finally my eyes swayed up a little on the screen.

I look up at the velvety blackness of the sky
And I see stars adorning nights dress so bright

Even diamonds may feel shy

And then I see one
That breaks free and shoots to
I know not where
Oh little star!
Will you take my wish to him who is so far
Tell him that I am
Just a little lonely here...

Another pause. Fifteen seconds this time, before I burst into tears. Never before had I cried like that. It was loud, euphoric and ecstatic. If you had heard me then, your ears would have gone numb. In decibels, I could beat every child that had ever bawled on this planet. Trust me, it was so damn loud. The tears seemed to be unstoppable; rather I didn't try to stop them.

I read the poem, once again, while tears still streamed down my face.

'Wow, she remembered my poem. She's not as mean as she looks.' The thought flashed in my mind. A strange chuckle followed. I looked at the mirror. With sticky cheeks, tearful eyes and a wide grin on my face, I was at my ugliest. But boy! I could stand my ugliness. Never before had it looked so beautiful to me.

'Boom!' A blaring sound rang through my room. Someone was banging on my door. I stopped adoring my impeccable beauty and wiped my face with whatever I could get hold of in my messy room. It was a pillow cover - dirty enough to streak my sticky face with dust but sufficient to absorb all my tears.

More pounding on my door and I could hear people shouting outside.

'What the hell are you doing inside Birthday Boy? It's not advisable to play with your self on the day you're born!' Anuj's twisted mind was at its best.

I opened the door. Anuj and Aryan were waiting for my divine presence.

'At least I've got something to play with, but poor you!' I grimaced at him and low-fived with Aryan, who was laughing.

'Whatever! So, what's up?' Anuj asked.

'Your face looks weird. Have you been crying all the while?' Aryan asked, after he noticed my face.

'No, nothing! It's the result of the facial that you guys gave me with my birthday cake.' I lied, my body language clearly giving them a hint of what I was up to.

'Go, wash your face. By the way, we are planning to get drunk today. What say?' Anuj said.

'No! I'm already intoxicated.' I said and went to the loo.

'But it's your day dude!' I heard Anuj shouting.

'Yes, indeed it's my day.' I yelled back.

When I returned back, intoxicated with the ecstasy I had experienced minutes ago, I didn't expect the prospective first-time wannabe drinkers to be around, but to my surprise Aryan was sitting in my room, playing with my souvenir – the ice-cream cone.

All the memories of my first and last date came back flooding in. The past seemed nearer than the present. In a moment, I got worked up. I so badly wanted to meet Tanya.

'Hey, don't play with it. It's personal.' I murmured to Aryan, trying my best to hide my loneliness. I had a tough time fighting my vulnerable state and was close to tears.

'Hey I never said sorry for what I did that day. Sameer told me what tragedy you'd faced that day.' Aryan said in a morose way.

That was least expected of Aryan. Come on, him being sentimental is like a cow eating bones. A handsome cow, I must say!

'Hey stop all this emotional bullshit, otherwise I would start crying. I am sorry too. I didn't even bother to speak to you guys after that day. I feel so disgusted with myself.' I said trying to avoid eye-contact with him owing to the slight embarrassment as well as the recent euphoria of getting my girl back. When two contrasting emotions are mixed, it makes you sick!

'What's wrong with you?'

'Everything is right. This is what is wrong with me!' I said and broke into tears.

Well, it isn't quite advisable to cry in front of your friends, especially, the ones who never miss opportunity to make fun of you. I was expecting a perfect dose of leg-pulling to come thereafter. But things were really right for me.

Aryan shook my shoulders and with a distinct concern in his voice, asked, 'You got her back?'

I didn't know whether my answer was going to be a yes or a no. Well, online rendezvous does not qualify as 'getting-someone-back.' And with the deadly villain like Tanya's mom, getting her back was like liberating Sita from Ravana's captivity. Unsure of the answer, I chose the easiest path out. The word called 'hmm'.

'Hmm.' I blurted.

It is funny how such an innately meaningless word could offer countless interpretations to the person it is directed at. Not that, it disorients the exact meaning, but it just offers plenty of other meanings at the same time. Now, it's upon the person to decide which meaning he chooses. Aryan, as written on his face, was smart.

'You mean you got her back.' Aryan said, his eyes shining with excitement.

'Yeah!' I exclaimed and I jumped to hug him. Well, that was just out of the blue. The hug was great – sharing joy is so gratifying, but at the same time, it was so damn awkward.

Let me tell you about 'hugs' in brief. Hugs – amongst men, is a subject worth discussion. There was a time when hug signified friendship, warmth and bonding. But, this was at the time when we were hanging around in our nappies. The nineties, you might say. As time progressed, and orientations digressed, men-hugging-men were seen in a new light – the light of awkwardness and in worst cases, obscenity. The gay rights movement brought freedom to this act of affection but at the same time, it made this act typically gay in the eyes of some.

'Wow, Himadri girls were so right!' A *treble-some* voice triggered interrupting our awkward manly hug midway. 'It's official now! Aryan is gay, and is in love with Kanav.' Anuj, the blabbermouth, could not refrain from mocking us for our public display of affection, in private. He ran across the hostel corridor to make sure that each and every guy would be an accomplice in his diabolical defaming task.

'Bloody asshole!' Aryan freaked out and ran behind the culprit. While I kept laughing, instead of being embarrassed. God! I missed this happiness so much.

All alone, with nothing other than Tanya's fond memories for company, I opened the laptop. I wanted to reply to her. Desperately, indeed.

I logged into my account, stared at the screen, just when my cell-phone buzzed. The mere sight of an unknown number set my heart pounding. Come on, it was 3 o' clock at night. The realization that it was an Indian number did lower it down a bit. Careful yet excited, in wishful anticipation, I picked up the phone.

'Happy Birthday handsome!' An abnormal female-voice said from the other-side. It wasn't her, the fake American accent could tell me clearly. Let us call the person on the other side – The Bitch, for the time being.

'Hi. Who's this?' I said, scandalized.

'Guess who? I've known you since last Feb. Don't you remember the birthday party, where we first met?' The Bitch squeaked.

I was in a fix. How the hell could this Bitch know about Ruchi's birthday party? Loud rowdy laughs as the background music answered my question.

'Oh yes, I do remember. How have you been Smriti?' I begun, now the hearts pounded on the other side.

'Smriti? I am not any Smriti.' The Bitch said in a worried voice. Now my confusion was transferred effectively to the other side, as I could hear some pounding hearts, among masculine voices.

'Oh, how come you don't remember? We made out in the washroom of that restaurant, that day. Oh I forgot that you were drunk.' I said and set forward towards the kennel, where The Bitch was hiding with other dogs.

'Now I do remember. After all, you're the father of my son.' The Bitch said while the other dogs howled uncontrollably in the background. I entered the kennel – Sameer's room – where The Fat Bitch was talking to somebody named Kanav on the other side, looking outside the window.

'Oh! I want to screw you once more. Bitch!' I said and kicked Sameer's heavy butt hard. All the domestic animals wailed in jest.

'Ah!' Sameer shouted as he turned around, furious.

'Screwed!' I said.

'Totally!' Anuj echoed.

'Hey, the birthday boy is here. Aryan, bring out my 100 bucks. I won the bet.' Sameer said. His eagerness could have rivaled a dog eyeing a juicy bone. Aryan took out a 100 rupees note. I was confused.

How could losing a prank count as winning a bet?

'What bet?' I questioned.

'Oh! Coming back from your room, I told these scoundrels that Kanav would not join the *daru-party* since it's his day today,' Aryan said with a wink, and continued, 'and this fat-ass made a bet, that he would call you without even asking you. And you rascal, did you not have some very important work right now?'

'Well, I have but I find this bitch on the phone sexier.' I said looking at Sameer. He got me.

'What? You got your girl back?' Sameer said; his eyes dilated while his jaw fell. Anuj and the other hostel mates were also gaping in awe, wonder, and a little digust as though I had committed a horrendous crime by having a girlfriend.

I nodded, with a brace-full of smile on my face. The response was quite unexpected – unrestrained howling. Little did I know that even men could howl like wolves. My already tormented butt was subjected to more kicks. However, my outcry outdid their howling, which somehow managed to gratify my tormented soul.

'What? When? How?' Sameer and Anuj exclaimed together, in resonance.

'What better reason do you need to party? Start off the party dude!' Aryan interrupted in between and played 'Linkin Park' aloud on the speakers. All of their curiosity sublimated in the joy of rock, on the rocks.

I was waiting for them to ask me my story, but instead, they kicked off the fiesta. I felt bad for a while, but suddenly 'The Linkin Park Baba' sang in my years 'in the end, it doesn't even matter,' and I felt at ease. It seemed that God communicated to me through them.

I uttered to myself, 'fair enough,' and joined the group. The ecstasy on their faces seemed to be telling me that my happy times had come. Aryan took out bottles from his bag – rum, vodka and whiskey. If it had been an earlier version of me, I would have run a thousand miles away just at the mere mention of these 'bad-words', but with time, I got acclimatized to *dilli-ki-hawa* and now I exhibited a mature indifference to them. Sticking to my small-town roots, I hadn't ever dared to touch them, just because it was way out of my comfort zone. But now seemed the time to be high; God gave me everything I could have ever wished for.

The bottles were opened; the drinks were served with ice. Anuj brought packs of kurkure, chips and other snacks from his room. Sameer straightaway jumped on the snacks – quite understandable, looking at his ravishing figure. Anuj took two shots of neat vodka directly, with two other skinny drunkards, namely Manas and Samarth.

Aryan poured vodka in two glasses and walked towards me. I got nervous. Never before had I been offered a drink. You know, considering the kind of guy I am. With every step that Aryan took towards me, my feet turned colder and colder.

He came to me and offered one of his glasses to me. I declined. He offered again. I declined again. He offered again. I accepted. It does not seem good to decline something which your friend offers you, especially if your mind is a little bit dicey.

What would be the first thing you would have done if you were to hold a tumbler full of vodka for the very first time in your life? Well, you might taste it. Or you might smell it. Or at least just look at it. But not me. I closed my eyes, turned off my olfactory senses, deadened my taste buds and straightaway gulped it down – in one go. It burnt my throat, scorched my food-pipe and my stomach was on fire, instantly.

'Cheers to Kanav,' Aryan shouted. Everyone cheered.

'Yuck!' I said and barfed out everything – in one go. The party suddenly became numb, more precisely mum. A moment later, seeing my splatter, two more guys followed my example. The smell of vodka was soon overshadowed by something more disgusting.

'Fuck' and 'yuck' reflected the mood of the party. The result – the venue of the fiesta changed from Aryan's room to the Gentleman-of-the-day, alias Kanav's.

Well, hosting a *daru-party* after puking out every damn molecule of *daru* from your body is not something hearty, especially, when your mind revolves around your long-lost girlfriend who might be waiting desperately to hear from you on the other side of the globe. But can you resist your friends if they are drunk and wild? Well, you might, but you won't, because you yourself don't want to miss the fun.

So, here I was – my laptop packed, my table tidied up to let bottles and glasses reside there for sometime. The gang came up and settled themselves on my bed. Sameer had already had three pegs of vodka and was woozy. Aryan, being experienced, was however in control. Anuj was nowhere to be seen, he happened to disappear from the scene, together with his scrawny friends. The best thing that happened to me after I barfed out everything was that now no-one wanted to offer me another drink.

'Hey, Anuj is sleeping here.' A short geek named Kshitij shouted from some place, which we couldn't figure out at first. A couple of more screams later, it became clear that it was the place where nature was in abundance, with its different calls.

'He is sleeping with his chin stuck to the commonde. And he has puked as well!' Kshitij shouted, scandalized. The first *daru* party had its effect on drinkers and non-drinkers alike. Those who drank got senseless while those who didn't couldn't believe their senses as to what had happened.

We dragged Anuj to my room. Somebody brought a lemon from the mess and his intoxication fizzed away to some extent. Everybody settled with their glasses on my bed. There was pin drop silence. It lasted for so long that we became restless that someone would break it. Almost all of us seemed to suffer from 'the-next-man-will-do' syndrome, when the bulkiest one amongst us decided to steer the task.

'Bloody bitch, I'll kill her.' Sameer screamed abruptly.

Well, it's funny when you hear a big fat chubby guy, all drunk and all sentimental, taking out his entire frustration caused by an unsuccessful fling. No matter how hard you try, you can never sympathize with a big guy, his frustration triggers laughter – to the drunk and non-drunk soul alike.

'What happened big boy?' Aryan asked.

'You know that girl Reva, don't you?' Sameer asked all of us.

'Of course I remember. I used to bluff desperate guys in our early classes by sending absurd songs and lewd pictures through Bluetooth, using her name. Their expressions were really shocking after that, since they would turn towards Reva and give her lecherous stares.' Anuj said with pride.

'Wow!' I exclaimed, amazed. Anuj's innovative endeavours were really a shocker, since I had no idea about them.

'Yes, the same one. That girl screwed all my plans.'

'What plans?' Anuj asked, half drowsy, half awake. I realized what plans.

'Oh, I was going to propose to her!'

'What?' Aryan spilled some of his Bacardi on the floor as he shouted. There could not have been a better way to molest my pure and untouched room. I kept mum, since there was something that bothered me more than the splatter.

How could my ingenious scrabble proposal idea fail? Sameer must have blundered.

'Dude, are you out of your senses? Reva – didn't you get anybody better?' Aryan started his all-time 'there-is-a-glamorous-world-outside-IIT' preaching. As expected, infatuated, frustrated and intoxicated Sameer had no ear for all this.

'Screw you and your I-am-the-God-of-you-all attitude. Have a life of your own dude. You got a better one, don't you? So you go and bloody...' Sameer lost his temper.

'Stop it.' I interrupted before the duel worsened. There is a thing about being drunk – everything goes on a high – your joy, your emotional state as well as your temper. The only thing that remains on ground or goes further down is your grades.

'Sameer, what happened to your proposal? Did you try the scrabble one?'

'Dude, I tried and failed miserably. She kicked my butt.' Sameer said in a sympathy-seeking tone.

'What's this scrabble proposal?' Aryan asked us. Everyone seemed curious.

'Oh, it's Kanav's brainchild. This sucker would explain that.' Sameer transferred the explanation work to me, while he drank listlessly.

'Take your girl to Barista – where they've got scrabble; get her something to eat while you go and fetch the scrabble. When you bring the game board with all the alphabets, shuffle the alphabets in the bag and keep I, L, O, V, E, Y, O and U in your fist and hide the alphabets T, O, O in your pocket. Keep your fist inside the bag, so that when you come back, you could yourself take out the alphabets for her and define the rules of the game – that one has to come up with phrases, instead of words. Done with the phase one, await for her to lay down the most endearing phrase of your life – and then put the T, O, O after that. And say the damn thing. The girl is floored and you are an achiever.' I said, with a slight pride in my voice. My engineering mind did engineer something novel.

'Oh, ho ho! A hell of a technique it is. Dude, I can't believe it's the same dumbass Kanav who came up with something as amazing as this. I'm gonna try this soon.' Anuj said out of the blue, partly unconscious. Well for me, I took Anuj's comment as a compliment. Seldom had I got any compliment, so the distinguishing parameter didn't seem to exist in my case.

'Go for it dude, would love to see you screwed, like me.' Sameer remarked. Clearly, something was wrong. Somebody had a story to tell.

'What happened fatty? Tell us the whole thing.' I asked Sameer.

Suddenly Sameer's face lit up. All his alcohol induced drowsiness was flushed down. In his typically drunken wavering but excited voice, he began his story.

'Well guys, here goes your entertainment – my tragic love story, where everything seemed right until the word love came into it.' He said dreamily.

Isn't it amazing that while reciting one's sad tale, a person forgets his sadness for the time being?

'It all started after that mall incident,' Sameer started his tryst with love, 'when I first talked to Reva, I had developed a special feeling for her. In just those 15 minutes that I spent with her, while bringing the birthday cake, I could feel that she was the one. She was totally similar to me – in thinking, in beliefs and ideals, and in ...'

'In shape...' Aryan squeaked, creating a perfect LOL condition, thus disturbing our storyteller's intense articulation. We all somehow prevented our laughter from bursting out.

'Yeah, whatever, you dog! If you're not interested in listening to my story, kindly get your ass out of here,' Sameer continued while Aryan zipped his lips, opening his mouth occasionally, only to sip his drink, 'So, where was I, you suckers? Yes, so speaking about that bitch. She was ... bloody ... yeah, she was totally similar to me – in everything. Yes, even in shape. That's why I was so fond of her. You know why I didn't go for any girl during socials, because I was inwardly committed to Reva, and I would never give way to infidelity.'

'This asshole asked 10 girls for dance during socials, and got rejected by all of them. Now listen to the love guru talking about commitment.' Aryan whispered in my ear.

'Awww...so sweet!' Aryan commented sarcastically. This time Sameer didn't reciprocate and continued with the story.

'After the mall incident, courtesy you guys, my entire dream world shattered. There was no communication on the girl's side for entire two months. And neither did you guys take any initiative. After all, you people got committed thereafter while I was left all alone. Last semester, I occasionally chatted with her over the net, but she didn't pay me any attention. As soon as I came back from vacations, I started bridging the gap. I got to know that Reva used to go for Salsa classes, in Saket…'

'Dude, don't tell me that you joined Salsa classes.' Anuj said.

'I should not have but I did. I joined. It was a 10 days crash course. A hell of a bad dancer that I'm, it could not have been worse. For the first three days, I was an object of ridicule for everybody, including Reva, but then I caught the rhythm. We didn't get to talk, since our dance partners would be shuffled alphabetically everyday, and our dance partners were who we spent most of our time with. I had to wait for 9 days to have Reva as my partner, since luckily on the last day we were assigned to each other. That was the day; we danced – my left hand on her waist and her right hand on my shoulder, the other two hands holding each other's. It was a bit awkward for her, since we didn't talk at all after that mall incident in the first year. But once with her, I didn't wait and I initiated…'

'Initiated chattering.' Aryan whispered into my ear. I sniggered. I shouldn't have, but I couldn't resist. Shit happens, you know. Sameer stared at me, took his glass of vodka and left the room.

His story was progressing so wonderfully that we could not wait to guess what happened next. All of us ran after him, some being so painfully drunk that they smashed into the wall as they encountered it. Some, who were a bit alert, dashed into the big guy as they saw him. He got more flustered.

'You guys go and enjoy yourselves in the room. I'm also enjoying myself here, toasting with the moon.' Sameer said and drank the whole peg in one go.

He was angry – fine. But he was throwing tantrums – not fine.

Throwing tantrums is a very tricky business. It needs experience, knowledge and expertise to practise it. It's appreciated only when the receiver is a person from the opposite sex and he/she is sympathetic; but if the receiver happens to be a person of the same sex and that too ruthless friends like us, trust me, the donor becomes the receiver.

Sameer was standing in the balcony, enjoying a toast with the moon. It was such a delightful toast that he decided to tell the rest of his story to us standing there, until his legs gave up. After massaging Sameer's huge ego with two glasses of whiskey, we persuaded him to continue with his epic love story in my room.

'So you initiated chattering, what after that…' I taunted Sameer.

'Yes smut-bag, I began chattering. I apologized for what had happened that day, and made it pretty clear that I had no evil intentions behind it. We began talking. She didn't open up initially, but things smoothened thereafter. We travelled back to IIT together and had a delightful chat. At the end, she asked me about Aryan's orientation and I confirmed that he indeed was gay.' That was Sameer's way of taking revenge. He outshone each one of us. This time Aryan too didn't bounce back.

'And then?' One of us asked. Clearly the story was getting engrossing, since this time no-one carried on the hoaxing ceremony.

'Did you ask for her phone no.?' I asked; the reminiscence of my first chat with Tanya came alive.

'No, it was too early for that. So coming back to where we were, the Salsa classes were now over, we have had our first outing and Aryan was officially gay. Things remained the same. I started following her on the social network and added her personal id in my chat list.'

'So basically, you were … bloody stalking her. She's bloody hot, I testify to that. I've seen her … she's bloody damn hot.' Anuj said, his intoxication following a sinusoid, this time reaching the crest of it. The state of complete insobriety brings some mind-blowing effects in different people. In case of Anuj, it made him more ferocious with blood splattering out of his mouth in the form of 'bloody' prefixed to every single word.

'Thanks Anuj. We all know that you know the temperature profiles of every girl on the planet. Nothing could have been more pleasing than your testimony.' Sameer boomed.

'Take care of yourself, you are full.' Aryan advised Anuj, who was totally out of his mind. He hopped around like a frog at one time and at other times, would sit like a tortoise with a single expression on his face. Now he was lying with his dopey face pushed against the pillow, which was mine. His butts jumped once in a while, thereby letting us know that he was still awake. That's what alcohol does to you. It makes a monkey out of a man.

'So you added her in your chat list?' Manas provoked our storyteller. Before going on a bit further, let me tell you about Manas.

Manas was a fun guy; seen with books during days and cigarettes, with occasional weed, at night. His life had two passions: academics and narcotics. He was such a heavy smoker that once he accidentally slept with a cigarette tucked in his lips and his bedsheet caught fire.

Thank god that his weed buddies were around, they immediately took control of the situation. His is a different kind of story – a very interesting one, but we would delve into it later, since our fleshy storyteller is waiting impatiently to relate his.

'Finally, someone seemed interested,' Sameer began. I wondered where all the alcohol had gone since he didn't seem intoxicated at all. I presumed his big tummy was the answer. Or his excitement as he held on to his most desired position – of a speaker. He must have waited for this day for long, since his *pravachanas* have had no listeners lately. The best part was that this time there was no speck of philosophy in his words; perhaps life had given him a practical lesson.

'Yes, so I added her in my chat list. The first time I pinged her, she took a long time to reply, but I waited. To love is to wait, I thought.' he said, this being the first tinge of philosophy that struck my ears that night. Well, not too bad, rather real good. I could also second his last line.

'So I waited. For half an hour before she replied to my *hi*. But she replied. And what followed was three hours of non-stop chatting.'

'Chattering.' Aryan remarked with a wink.

'We talked about several things, including Aryan's orientation. We both were sorry about you, Duke!' Sameer teased Aryan and continued, 'anyhow, and these chats soon moved on to the phone. It was intense, overwhelming and totally out-of-this-world. Day before yesterday, I asked her out on the pretext that I needed to buy something for my sister and I needed a girl to accompany me to the garment shop because I have no frigging idea about what looks good and what's not.'

'Rather who looks good and who doesn't.' Aryan, by now a little inebriated, looked tired while commenting.

'True. Now would you let me go ahead or not. I'm damn sleepy and I am also full, if you people interrupt me once again, off goes my tragedy and your lives become tragic thereafter.'

'Sure, continue.' Aryan, for the first time, succumbed. Anuj, by this time, was off to sleep, with his face still kissing my pillow. Manas, who restrained himself from a puff or two because it being my room, also seemed to desperately wait for the end of the story.

'I was planning for the scrabble proposal. Everything was perfect. We went to the Shopper's Stop, we liked a dress, she even tried it – she was looking stunning in it – so ravishing that I wanted to buy it for her instead. After that, we went to Barista. And that's where the disaster occurred.'

'What – coffee fell on her?' I asked.

'Did she fall for any guy at Barista?' Manas asked, with a pen in his mouth. It was quite clear from his body language that he was missing a cigarette, and he would have even chewed his own thumb if not stopped.

'The scrabble proposal failed. It failed miserably.'

'What?' I yelled, loud enough to make Anuj turn his face sideways.

'Yes, that blockhead made a bloody fool out of me and your idea.

I ordered two 'Dark Temptations' for both of us and once served, I
went to fetch the game. Done with all the prerequisities, I returned
and started the game. When I gave her the alphabets I, L, O, V, E, Y,
O, U; she thought for a while and made an 'EVILYOU' out of those.'

'Oh crap! I didn't even think about it.' I said, stupefied.

'Ha-ha-ha,' a loud riotous laughter emerged from my pillow. It
was Anuj. 'Gosh! This is the funniest tragedy ever. Oh my God, ha-
ha-ha. What a bloody climax!' Anuj exclaimed and again crouched
down on the pillow, laughing uncontrollably. Surprisingly enough,
he was awake all this while. Aryan joined the laughing gang, and I
too could not stay lag behind.

'And that's not all. After a moment, that bitch says that "oh, I've
realized something amazing, this could also be made into I-love-you,
what an awesome way of proposal it would be if someone tries it?
I'm going to try it on Siddharth, the next time he comes to meet
me." I was stunned. I didn't have the guts to ask her who Siddharth
was. She herself burnt my soul when a minute later she said, "Oh, I
forgot to tell you about Siddharth. Siddharth is my boyfriend, who
lives in Mumbai. We got committed on phone last month, we've
not yet met. It was for him that I started learning Salsa, since he
dances really well." There could not have been a better way to break
someone's heart.'

'What a bloody loser! There could not have been a better end to
this bloody day. Ha-ha-ha, awesome! I've not heard a more kick-ass
bloody tragedy before. Ha-ha.'Anuj exclaimed and with my help,
got up from the bed.

'Some of your bad-luck got induced to me. Don't you remember your days of Niti caught you red-handed when you went on a date with her roommate?'

'Oh that was bloody intentional. I wanted to bloody get rid of that fat irritating dunce. She was a bloody pain in the ass. Always wanting me to bring her bloody presents or talk 'cute' on the phone. Who tolerates such bloody nonsense?' Anuj said in his bloody intoxicated tone. He was now standing, bleary-eyed and kept swaying around a little, when I took charge of accompanying him to his room. He stank. He stank big-time. He collapsed thrice on the way back; I helped him get up in the first two times, but left him on the floor the third time.

I sat down, slapped him twice; when he gained a little of his bloody senses, I shouted at him, 'Why the hell do you drink so much?'

His reply was classic. 'It bloody forces me to take bath the next day, which otherwise would be weekly.'

'Wow, you seem to be in your senses. Get up.' I dragged him to his room, sprayed some of his perfume over him and over myself as well; went back to my room, where the crowd was supposedly still waiting for me. On the way back, Manas bid adieu to me, with a smile holding his beloved cigarette. When I returned to my room – Sameer and Aryan were gone. The empty bottles, the shabby bed and sullied floor did no good to my birthday ego. But, I was grateful to everyone around, including God –I spent the next fifteen minutes cleaning up the whole mess.

It was 5.15 am in the morning. Enervated, I lay down straight on my back on the bed, thinking about the last five hours, absorbed in the mental tug-of-war.

'What if she's been waiting for my reply all the while? Oh no, she hates social networking websites so much, she wouldn't be loitering around. What if she is indeed waiting? No, she can wait. Should I reply now, yes, I should get up now … or in just a minute…umm…zzz.'

And then, there was no light.

Sleep is a funny thing. When it takes over, everything else becomes secondary, even your long-lost, newly found love. When my eyes opened, I was in a fix, as though amnesia had cursed my memory. I looked across the room; the smell of my 'inebriated' pillow cured my memory loss in one go. The moment I looked at my watch, I wanted to mark my birthday as my death anniversary. I slept not eight hours, not nine, but ten hours straightaway. It was 3.30 pm.

10 out of 24 hours on bed, on your birthday, that too with no one for company – what a sheer waste of time! I got up, angry and with my partially-glued eyes, I sat down in front of my laptop. Every second that went by escalated my anger, until finally, I logged into my Orkut account. It took me four tries to get the password right – *alldayidreamabouttanya* – since in my excitement, I typed only one 't' in "abouttanya" every single time.

Pissed, I shuffled through the pages of my scrapbook, the number of scraps quadrupled from midnight, until I reached the awaited scrap.

Nothing has changed but still I stared at it like a child. I clicked the 'reply' button and poured my heart down.

I hate you. I hate you. I hate you. But, I love you. I don't know why I do? But I do.

I want to beat you, slap you and hug you at the same time. Where have you been? This is not fair at all. You cannot just run away from me. I am not just any other guy. I mean, how could you resist talking to me for so long? Didn't you miss me? Thank God that my birthday was so near. What if my birthday had been on a leap-year's 29th February? Would you have waited for four years to reach out to me? And yes, it's nice that you remembered my poem, but let me tell you it is not going to make me happy. You are the one who is going to keep me happy. I am tired of being lonely.

Oh my God, I feel like crying. I know I look ugly when I cry, but I seriously can't help. This time, you are making me cry. I hate you. You're a bigger jerk than I am, do you understand? And I don't want to play scrabble with you. You go to hell. Just go to hell. Well, you would be pleased to know that thanks to you, there has been a welcome change in me - I have started hating this thing called social networking. I hate typing this letter to you. I hate this virtual world. I want my real world back. I want you back. I want to hear your voice. Why couldn't you call me? I want to see you; my eyes have become tired of living in make believe world.

Do not leave me for so long that I stop missing you.

I finished penning my emotional outburst. I read the reply two times, smiled in expectation of a reply three times and furrowed my eyebrows with a concealed helplessness once. I went on to click on the 'Post Scrap' tab.

'Your scrap cannot be created.'

This was what appeared while the entire scrap vanished. God, I hated it.

When you've experienced one oops moment in your life, others don't quite wait to follow up. The smiles that embellished my face previously seemed to me a complete waste of time. Well, what more to expect from a kiddo' who has been totally unaware of the virtual world? The default auto-privacy option of Orkut blocked scraps from unknowns, and she hadn't sent me a friend request either to enable me to *create* the damn scrap. I, on the other hand, to allow girls from my school to reach out to me, had set the privacy barrier to nil.

The only thing I could do was to type the entire scrap once again and this time, send it instead as a message. The whole intensity of my emotions was washed away. Disinterestedly, I went ahead to craft my next sentimental letter. I remembered a few of the things that I had written earlier. Relying on my short-term memory, I began, but midway, I got bored. I chose the road of fun – the road that I had missed for one long month because of that technologically impaired girl.

~~I hate you. I hate you. I hate you. But, I love you. I don't know why I do? But I do. I want to beat you, slap you and hug you at the same time.~~

25

Thanks for your birthday wishes. By the way, who's this? I went through your profile but could not decipher your identity.

To be frank, I've tried that scrabble trick on many girls, so I am sorry that I can't clearly remember. And yes, your profile shows one of my poems. Well, that's sweet. As far as I remember, I had given that poem to just three girls – Shambhavi, Smriti and Dhara. Let me take a wild guess – are you, by any chance, Shambhavi, since she likes to call me jerk?

The good news is that I am single nowadays. I dumped that irritating dunce Tanya a month ago. It feels like heaven, now. Hope to see you someday, Shambhavi. We would hang out and hang 'in' as well, if time permits.

Do reply. Waiting to hear from your side. Take care.

P.S. Wanna have butterscotch? :P

That was it. I sent the message and heaved a laughter-filled-sigh. A strange realization struck my mind. Humour, that's what brings me happiness. I could expel all signs of sorrow by using this powerful weapon.

The next two hours were uneventful. Apart from my sitting in front of the laptop in hope of getting reply from the-lady-of-the-hour for one hour, I attended a couple of calls from *Prakriti* and a dozen of phone calls from relatives, some of them so distant that I couldn't even recall their faces. Well, that's what being an IITian does to you if you're from an ordinary middle class family.

My friends tried their best to persuade me to give them a treat, but I somehow managed to sneak out of the hostel. I had to meet Ruchi.

Ruchi and I had become more of birthday-friends; we had not met after her birthday. Other than the occasional calls that we had made to each other, in relation to Tanya after our first-and-last date, I hardly ever talked to Ruchi after I got committed. Love divides and rules, you see.

I was looking forward to meeting her. After all, I had news to share with her.

We decided to meet at Dilli Haat, a place rich in colours and antiquities, famous for its variety of good food. I left my hostel early, just to get rid of the nettling company of my hungry broke friends, and reached the Haat at around 6.45 pm. Ruchi was supposed to come at 7 pm, so I had 15 minutes to kill. Entry inside the place required a ticket, so I had no option other than to stroll outside its entry point, assessing and analysing the facts and figures of the things around – facts about the history of the place and figures of, oh come on, you know what.

A group of foreigners flocked towards the entry point, eagerness quite visible on their white faces. I was drawn towards the activities of a young blonde kid, around five years of age, who was trying his best to attract the attention of the crowd around, by making sounds of animals, every now and then. Quite a talented kid, I must say. A huge commotion occurred when the same kid intentionally pinched the bum of a young Indian girl and disappeared behind his father, who was presumed to be the culprit by the victim. It was fun. I was perpetually smiling, thoroughly entertained and slightly envious, since somewhere deep down, despite being supposedly a decent guy, I wanted to be that boy's place – for the sheer fun of it.

'Hey Geeko, What are you staring at?' Somebody whispered in my ear. Ruchi.

'Hey Silly, how have you been?' I almost screamed, with pleasure – the pleasure of meeting your friend after a long time. We hugged; a short one though.

'I am awesome. I thought you knew it.' She said.

'Yes, of course I know. How is everything else?' I said.

How is everything else? This is perhaps the most useless but yet most used question in human history. First, it does not define what comes under the category of 'everything else' – it's up to the person to perceive what exactly you mean by it. And secondly, the answer to it is already known to you. Almost certainly. In 99 percent of the cases, the answer is 'everything else is fine', despite things being not-so-fine in some. In the remaining one percent, where the things are completely screwed up and the other person needs a waterfall of sympathy to bathe, s/he says, 'Things are not well', when you question dramatically with utmost concern, which most of the times is fake, 'What happened? Tell me, what happened.' Well, I had no innovations in my mind so I went with the stereotype.

But Ruchi's answer was different – different enough to be called different. 'When you're awesome, who cares about everything else?' She said.

I was pleased. We bought the tickets, which was priced 20 rupees for the Indian citizens and 400 rupees for the foreigners – a clear sign that Indian economy was on a high – 20 INR had a value of 400 rupees for the foreigners. Productive discrimination!

Anyhow, coming out of my Geeko self, I escorted Ruchi to the entrance of the Haat. My eyes were looking for the bottom-pincher *firang* all the while.

'How is "everything else" at your side?' Ruchi asked, stressing on the clichéd phrase.

'It's awe……summer.' I said with a wink.

'What do you mean?' She said, perplexed. Having lost one's first love, you don't expect the person to be filled with such joy.

'Oh, I got committed once again. A girl from my college.'

'What?' She shrieked.

'Yes, didn't I tell you about Sushmita?' I asked in all seriousness.

'Sushmita?' Ruchi questioned, getting all worked up.

'Yes, Sushmita. She's a fresher at IIT, and yes, she's quite a delight.'

'What?' Ruchi freaked out. The expression on her face constantly reflected a question mark. She winced and furrowed her eyebrows.

'First look at your face and then dream. Not everyone is as foo… I mean nice as Tanya to fall for you.'

'Oh certainly. Like you, Tanya, being your friend, has really been a foo…I mean nice.' I taunted and moved ahead.

We went inside the Haat, without talking much. The security guard at the entry gate tried his best to molest me, making sure that everything inside my clothes was non-metallic and original.

'Silly, I've to tell you something.' I said in a serious voice.

'Yes, say. You've been acting weird.'

'Yes, I am. But it's justified. After all that fool is back into my life. She wished me happy birthday on internet.'

'What? Are you kidding me?' Ruchi said, stunned.

'Why would I be kidding? I am not fond of giving myself false hopes.'

'Really? So the velvety blackness of the skies and diamonds that feel shy have finally arrived in your life. How is she?' She taunted.

I was scandalized. *Was she operating her account? Was Tanya around? How does she know about my poem? Is it Tanya wearing Ruchi's mask? Or vice-versa.*

The bright red nail-paint assured me that it was not Tanya. But my other doubts still clouded my mind.

'How do you know that?'

'What?'

'Those were the lines from the poem that I wrote for Tanya.'

'I know.'

'That's what I'm asking. How do you know that?'

'She showed it to me a long time back. I remembered those few words, I just repeated. You're amazing with words, by the way.'

'Stop it. I know it all now. You're operating that Orkut account just to please me. Aren't you? You're playing with me, I know. I mean how could you?'

'What account are you talking about?'

'The account from which she sent me a birthday wish. Just admit that you're the one behind it. Stop playing with me.' I whimpered, standing still. I was occasionally shivering and streaks of sweat crawled down my head as if they had waited all this time to sense that gravity pulls you down.

'What rubbish are you talking about? What account?' She acted as if I was talking Hebrew in front of her. I was literally pleading, with my legs shivering badly. Seeing my situation, her serious face cracked up into a smile.

'I hate you. How could you play with my emotions?' I whined, helplessly.

'Dude! Listen, nobody is playing with your emotions. I just went through your profile yesterday and saw her scrap as well as profile. I knew that no matter what happens, she would definitely contact you on your birthday.'

'How did you know?'

'Last year, on 19th Nov she had a very bad fight with her mother.'

'That's her birthday. What happened then? She never told me.'

'She wanted to take us to a discotheque on that day, after we urged her a lot to have some fun in life, at least on her birthday. She even took permission from her Mom, but things didn't turn out as expected. Despite permitting her initially, aunty did not let her go at the last moment, when she found out that two of our friends Shikha and Sonali had brought their boyfriends along with them. Tanya pleaded a lot, but she didn't allow her and scolded her along with the other two girls. She cried a lot that day.'

'The next day when she met me, she said to me, "Never love anyone. When they disappoint you on your birthday, the whole goddamn world breaks." I could not say a word. She took it upon her to make birthdays of all of her friends as happy as possible. You remember my birthday party. Waikiki was her idea. What a delightful day it was!'

'What a delightful day it was!' I echoed, lost in reminiscence. The effect of earthly gravity faded and the sudden gush of wind ruffled against my hair. Quite soothing. Amidst the noise of diverse hawkers and colourful buyers, clanking footsteps of women with leather slippers and their naughty children, crying babies and their garrulous mummies, my heart experienced divine tranquillity. The face of my goddess adorned my vision, until she was made to vanish by a sudden pinch on my butt. I was brought back from my trance to the real world and almost automatically, my eyes traced the culprit – the blond kid running away from me, looking at me with a mischievous smile. His cuteness made me forgive him; the pinch was too hard to forget however.

'Are you back?' Ruchi asked.

'Oh yes, my back,' I exclaimed and then continued without any complaint about the little bottom-pincher, 'I mean yes, I'm here.'

'You were telling me about Tanya.' I said as we moved ahead across the hawker *gully* to the local food court.

'You don't know how friendly we were. Even before you met her, she knew about you. I told her about you. When I told her how naïve you were, she wanted to meet you. That's why I made a bet on my birthday to get the two of you introduced to each other. I didn't know that a chance meeting would result in getting her hooked to you.'

Hooked!

The word provoked an inherent self-hate pulse in me. The tragic recollection of the climax of my first date came to my mind and made a shiver of mortification run through me. It was not the hook-up part that brought such sudden self-gloom, rather the sheer feeling of being caught – 'hooked'.

I wish I could write more about the time spent in the Haat, but it turned out to be a place suited for couples – both young and the old. Other than appealing food and good-looking girls, there was nothing worth spending on. However, Ruchi proved to be a respite from the monotony of my hostel room and made sure that the evening was well-spent. In desolation, company always helps. But help until sustained continuously seldom proves to be useful.

2. The Middle

One, two, three ... the counting went on. Days passed soon until it hit a week. Seven days, without a reply. It was depressing. Wait – that's not something that lovers are good at. They're good at – love, that's it. I know it sounds cheesy, but it's true.

It was raining that night. I stood on the verandah of my hostel, where the rain lashed against my chest, soaking my shirt. My spectacles were in dire need of a wiper. I stood against the rain and the wind. The mild beatings soothed my heart. The raindrops gave me a silent company, in my loneliness. When clouds stopped crying, I went back to my room. I didn't feel like changing my shirt. I liked the feeling – being drenched in the fragrant rain. It was a hug in disguise, something that I had been waiting for so long. I sat down on my chair, wiped my hair and opened my laptop.

I was feeling poetic. The rain made me long more for her, the wait

was irrepressible. My soaked fingers ran across the keyboard and gave
birth to a poem. Love made me a poet!

Wait
Another lonely night
Ghastly!
Thunderous clouds just cried

Stars have gone to sleep
Exhausted
Shining besides mountain - so steep

I'm all alone
Waiting
For someone, my own

Memories come flooding
Trapped
Between the wrinkles – budding

The first time we ever met
Serendipity!
It was. It wasn't love, yet

Those serene eyes rested on mine
Enraptured,
I stood, as though I saw Divine

I began to say when you
Stopped.
Your finger on my lips - and dew

'Wait till midnight,' A whisper said
Anticipative,
I smiled while you left

I waited. Days. Months. Years.
Forty-five
The wait doesn't get over, here

The whisper haunts my life
Love
Betrays me every midnight

Old, withered and desolate
Hopeful
Of seeing those eyes again, I wait

I liked what I had written. No, not in the narcissistic way but in an emotional way. I felt attached to what I had written. Happy with self-satisfaction, I published it on my blog. Once published, I wanted people to read it. So desperately, that I was ready to pay people to read it.

I went online and could see Ruchi and Sameer online. I pinged them, asking them to read my work. Coming out of one's laziness just to hear what the other person has to say is a tough thing to do, but to my surprise, they easily complied. After all, it was the first time I was asking them to read anything written by me. I waited – waited to hear from them. They didn't reply in the next two minutes.

I was in a fix. Either they hadn't gone through it or else, they were not able to understand it at all. With my wet shirt already giving me occasional shivers, I was in no mood to wait anymore.

I wrote to both of them.

Cold, shivered and afraid
Hopeful
Of hearing some words again, I wait

The replies followed, one by one.

> *Ruchi: You creep! You're such a child. Don't miss her so much. Why didn't you tell me that you're not feeling good? I would have called you!*
>
> *I: How did you find the poem?*
>
> *Ruchi is offline. Messages you send to Ruchi will be delivered when she comes online.*

Bad luck at its best. I couldn't wait more.

> *I: BTW, now that you know that I'm sad, you can still call me. Good night.*
>
> *Ruchi is offline. Messages you send to Ruchi will be delivered when she comes online.*

Meanwhile, my dear fatty had his own take at my poem. He couldn't digest that I could write a poem.

> *Motu: It's good initially, but as you proceed, it seems that you're being tortured – no not by the poem but by the helplessness of the writer. If you had made it humorous and added a few interesting words such as longing and desire, that would have added the spark. By the way, why are you so sad?*
>
> *I: Well, you know the very fact that I've not used the interesting words like longing and desire makes me sad. Thank you for helping me.*
>
> *Motu: Anytime. I always like helping people learn.*
>
> *I(thinking): Bloody asshole! If I help him learn that he's an asshole, I'll not only like it. I'm gonna love it.*

I sat back. My shirt had dried partly, thanks to the fan. Other things that were drenched in rain-water remained as wet as they could have ever been, making me nervous that some rashes might erupt on my two cushiony hillocks later on. I changed. The wait was still on; with no reply whatsoever from the other side of the globe. I prayed inwardly that my not-so-interesting poem didn't turn prophetical. Forty-five years, I would not be able to wait for a girl for so long. Wait holds as long as no other girl gives me *bhav*.

I didn't try to publicize my sad poetry amongst fellow beings, sparing them or rather myself of their uncalled for sympathy or suggestions. I was bored. Bored of friends, love and being sad. I was missing something in my life. It was not someone, but it was something. It didn't take me long to realize that it was humour, that I badly needed. It was futile being a hopeless romantic. Love isn't about fretting over; it's about feeling alive forever.

I realized what kind of journey I wanted to go on. I wanted to write – my own love story – in the most hilarious way I could. At 2 o' clock at night, I took my laptop, placed it on my lap and started typing. One hour. Two hours. Three hours. I could hear the wall clock ticking for the next ten hours. I couldn't stop. I had lost my sleep. I'd rediscovered what love meant. Love means joy.

Drowsy, when I turned to look out of the window, the bright sunlight outside literally seared my eyes. 12 noon. I tried to stand but my head went topsy-turvy and I fell down on the floor, with a smile on my face. Smile of satisfaction. I'd completed five chapters of my novel – finishing around 13000 words in one go. My ear-to-ear smile soon found its place in a dream. I could see her walking towards me, dressed in a stunningly beautiful white dress, adorned with her impeccable shy laughter and mesmerizing eyes. My wait was over, it seemed. She came near me, and whispered, 'So, you've begun the love story.'

I moved my hands towards her, holding her tightly by her slender waist and spoke in whispers, 'So, you've begun our love story.' She looked into my eyes and said, 'Make sure you make me laugh, like you always do.' I wanted to talk to her. My sleep didn't give me any further opportunity. I was driven to a state of complete lull, complete darkness and complete stillness. It was the most comfortable sleep of my lifetime – the floor had its own charms.

I woke up relaxed. It was 7 pm. The only side-effect that sleeping on the floor had on me was that my fleshy-hillocks suddenly founds some nano-hills on them. Rashes, they don't mind disturbing a man in love. I wanted to continue my writing. I was bitten by the bug. No, I'm not talking about the ass-biter! I was bitten by the bug called story-telling. After the little harassment by the mess(y) food, it was time to date my love once again.

In a lonely room with a welcome silence, I made love to MS-Word for the next 12 hours. This time, her parting words in my last night's dream acted like magic for me. When I wrote next, it was just an effort to make her laugh. No wonder, the effort seemed effortless. Her laughter was my life. In the process, there came several moments where the contagious bug called laughter affected me, when I used to sit back and laugh out loud at things that I'd written. The second writing streak enabled me to hit 25000 words milestone. The story was flowing at the speed of my thought. The thoughts were moving at the speed of light. Tired of sitting in the same position for the last 12 hours, I decided to take a break. I went to Anuj's room, for a little chitchat. He was playing Need for Speed on his almost-dilapidated laptop. The escape key had escaped his keyboard while the shift keys had been shifted to I know not where.

'Hey Kanav, what's up? Where have you been buddy, it has been days since I last saw you.' Anuj said, seeing me enter his room. His voice was excited, more because of the game than my tired face.

'I'd been in my room for the last three days.' I uttered. Every single word took me a lot of effort. I was enervated; it was just that sleep was miles away.

'Aha! Jerking off in solitude?' He said with a wild smile, turning his head towards me.

'No. Making love in solitude.' I replied.

'Fuck! Bloody sucker.' Anuj exclaimed. His next door neighbour squeezed his Carrera GT Coupe against the wall situated near the bridge on the Cote'd Azur track. He finished last. Quite a disappointment, I must say. Agitated, he punched his laptop keys with his fists. The computer made some eerie sounds and then automatically shut down.

'Wow.' I said, impressed with his command over the device.

'Ha! Yes, so who were you making love to, honey?' Anuj asked, flexing his bamboo like biceps against the mirror.

'Ah, it was Bill Gates' offspring. What a night it was!'

He turned around, shocked, 'Don't tell me that you did it with a CD-rom or something!'

'Shit! Shut the fuck up, asshole! I was writing the entire night – MS Word, does it ring a bell?'

'Oh…okay. By the way, what were you writing – a research paper? Or messages to random girls on Orkut?'

Let me remind you, in case you've forgotten, that it is 2008, the year when Orkut seemed to be the biggest invention of the mankind, and only a few people were converted into a bookworm by Zuckerberg.

'No baby, I'm not as gifted as you think to accomplish either of the tasks. I was just writing a novel.'

'Novel? Are you kidding?' Anuj said, with a constipated look on his face.

'What?'

'Man, come on! Writing a novel is not a child's play. My elder brother tried to write one. After months of futile efforts, he could not carry it on for more than four thousand words.' Anuj tried to convince me.

'That's because he lacked inspiration. In my case, I've crossed 25.'

'2500?'

'25000! In the last two days.' I said. He was gaping at me.

'What's it about?' Anuj asked. He was visibly excited.

'My love story.'

'Wow! Show me your novel. I want to read it.' He went towards my room. I lifted my debilitated body up just to prevent him from reading my work.

'Not until I finish. Until I finish making love, there'll be a do not disturb tag on my door. Hope you won't spoil my honeymoon.' I said, spoiling his enthusiasm.

'Hey, will you please write my love story?'

'Sorry, I said I'm writing a love story. Not a lust story. Nor an infatuation tale.' I taunted.

'Hey come on, it'll make it interesting. Make sure you don't change my name.'

'Hmmm. I'll see.' I said. My eyes were half-closed, silently echoing my words "I'll see."

'No, promise me now.' He said at my door.

'Ok, I promise. Good night.' I said, without realizing the implication of my promise and succumbed to the weariness.

My deep sleep was disturbed by the persistent sound of murmurs outside my room. As soon as I started gaining my senses, I realized that there were frequent knocks too. From inside the room, it seemed that a multitude of press reporters were waiting outside my room to take my interview. I combed my hair, thinking about interviews and the little fame. But alas! They were the same old curious-bunch – my batchmates.

'Hey Kanav, we heard that you're writing a novel. What's it about?'

One of the guys, Shailesh, whose face resembled the actor Mehmood's said.

'Oh, it's nothing of that sort. I have this habit of writing a diary. That's what I'm writing, rather compiling.' I realized that Anuj was my publicity agent. I didn't want any publicity with the task incomplete. I started lying. As a writer, you don't feel conscious while lying, since most of your time is spent in distorting the truth to make it more interesting and appealing to the readers.

'Come on, don't lie. We all know that you're writing a novel.' Rahul, one of the biggest nerds of our batch, said. He was good at just two things – note learning and note earning – by writing for technical blogs.

'Okay, I am.'

'Great to hear that. Now give us a treat.' Anuj said.

'So here comes the hungry dog! Treat, for what?'

'Oh come on, we're going to publicise your work when it gets published.'

'What? I've no intentions of publishing it. I'm writing just to entertain myself and my... friends.' I fumbled at the last word.

'Oh ho, our dear author is writing for his girlfriend.' Anuj said. The hungry-dog gang howled.

I blushed. Meanwhile, one of our batch-mates, Ishan who was listening to all this from a distance passed a bitter remark, 'Nowadays, every second guy wants to be an author.'

I was taken aback and so were the friends at my door. I didn't want an uninvited criticism to try to butcher my wings, even before my first flight. Without wasting another moment, I replied, 'Nowadays, every second guy is talking about me.'

My friends booed the cynic down. The atmosphere, which became tensed, soon became lighter. Anuj cracked a PJ, in Sunny Deol's voice, 'I wouldn't have cracked this poor joke had there been money in my pocket', to divert our attention from the cynic to the mimic. It took us some time to understand what he meant. I can very well empathize with you, if you've not got the PJ till now.

'Haan, most importantly, make sure that you write an elaborate sex scene in your novel. I wouldn't read otherwise.' Anuj continued. He knew how to set the mood of the crowd right. It's simple: talk about sex.

'I second that.' One of the guys said.

'I third that. I fourth that....' It went on until each and every horny bastard present there n^{th} that. The group dispersed after that, leaving Anuj behind.

'Sure. I'll make Anuj the king of sex. Happy?'

'Not happy. Satisfied, writer saheb!' Anuj said and continued with a wink, 'Please consult me before writing my heroines in your novel, I'll give you the right names for them.'

'So that when the original ones discover explicit things written about them, I'm the one they sue. Isn't it?'

'*Oh teri*, I didn't think about that. I'll make their names subtle, don't worry!'

'I'll make their names funny. Don't you worry.' I said and went back to my living-cum-writing room.

I wasn't writing literature. Nor did I want to. I was writing to make her laugh. And more so, to make myself laugh. It had been days since I'd laughed heartily and writing for sure was a welcome change in my life. Sorrow leads either to depression or creativity. I was glad that it was the latter in my case.

As a writer I realized that the best way to fight sorrow is to exaggerate its root cause to such an extent that it becomes humour. I was good at exaggeration. Story-telling seemed to be something that I had a natural proclivity for. I enjoyed it.

The process of writing indeed distracted me from my irrepressible wait, which otherwise would have taken a lifetime to get over. It was not that I was not missing Tanya at all. It was just that my missing her was transformed into my creativity. Through my writing, I used to spend the entire day with her vicariously. Two weeks passed by, and my first child was ready to be born. On 21st September, 2008, the first draft of my novel was almost complete. That might seem unbelievable if you don't know what inspiration can do to your life.

I had not yet decided about the title of my book. I had just named it 'Kismat Disconnection', slightly inspired by a stupid movie of that time.

Once done with giving form to my imagination, it was time to get appreciation. It seemed that my beloved had already forgotten me, since her presence on the virtual world seemed non-existent, with no replies whatsoever, so I chose my friends to be my first readers. Aryan, being the very first. His views on my work mattered the most, since he just didn't know flattery.

I went down to his room, with the printed version of my creation in my bag and asked him, 'Hey buddy, need your help. Would you go through my novel critically?'

Aryan was stunned, and began by asking me, 'Do you think I would offer any good insights to your work? I don't know any literature.'

'Come on, it's no literature. It's just our story. I bet you would enjoy it.'

'Did you write something bad about me? Now, I'll have to read it.' Aryan said.

I took the printed manuscript out and placed it on his table. 'Wait a minute, wait a minute. Are you asking me to read this thick manuscript? Are you kidding me?' Aryan shrieked.

'Why, what happened?'

'I've never ever read any book before. Forget it I would never be able to finish it. I'm an ass when it comes to reading stuff.'

'Just start it, if you're not able to finish it I'll get to know what I want.'

'Well, that's weird. Keep it on my table.'

'Sure, and you don't have all the time in this world, make sure you return my manuscript by tomorrow. I'll get it proof read by a couple of more friends.'

'Dude, you're asking for too much. Who can finish over 200 pages in one day, that too a supposedly romantic novel?'

'I'll acknowledge you specially if it gets published.' I said.

'Oh wow, that's sexy. Make sure you give my phone number too along with it.' He joked.

'Sure.'

I returned to my room. I was satisfied. I had finished my novel with the last scrap of Tanya. I wanted to write an epilogue, with the hope of meeting her in the near future. I dreamt of meeting her at Waikiki once again. I incorporated that as the epilogue, in addition to the true stories of EVILYOU Sameer and the tragedies in the life of Anuj.

I logged into Orkut, opened her profile and read through her 'about me' once again.

The velvety blackness of the sky
Adorned with night sky so bright

...

The good thing that happened at that very moment was that I didn't feel like crying. The bad thing that occurred was that I wanted to scream. I am such a girl, you might think. I also think so. Actually, many a times I feel that I'm a lesbian caged inside a man's body. Coming back to where I was, yes, I wanted to scream. I wanted to tell her that I wrote our entire love story, with a little exaggerations, and I so desperately wanted her to read it.

I ran my eyes across her profile. She had no friends. No photos. No 'testis'(thank God, we've moved to facebook now!). No videos. But a dozen scraps! WTF!

I was dumbfounded. No friends, with default privacy setting so constricted that no-one would be able to create a scrap, and she was there, adorned with a dozen scraps. I clicked on her scrapbook. It opened, at the speed of lightning. What I saw would have been the greatest surprise of my lifetime. She was there, in all her beauty and aura, trying to make her voice reach the other part of the globe for the last three weeks, by scrapping on her own scrapbook!

'What the hell!' I finally screamed.

'God! Why did she have to be my girlfriend?' I cried too.

I started reading her scraps. Nothing in this world could have been more frustrating. She wasn't technically impaired, she was just dumb! I mean, how could anyone be so stupid – that too for three weeks straightaway?

The first message.

….. posted at 9.37 am, 29ᵗʰ August, 2008
Hey Jerk, are you going to reply or not?

In return to my message – containing Shambhavi, Smriti and Dhara – delivered to her on my birthday, she had a reply present in her scrapbook. Yes, she had been so silly to reply to my message through a scrap. I can appreciate your feelings but yes, I am madly in love with that very stupid girl. And I could die to witness another stupid act of hers.

Have you ever laughed and cried at the same time? I did, the very moment when I started reading her scrap.

..... posted at 10.40 pm, 30th August, 2008

Hi Jerk. You're trying to be very smart and witty. Why can't you leave that thing to me! Smartness doesn't suit you. It's a girl's trait. And wow, nice to hear about so many girls in your life. Hope they have had an equally good time while smooching you!

And yes I forgot to tell you that your irritating dunce is waiting to hang 'in' with you. She'll make sure you hang till ants start wearing pants, while she would kick your ass so badly that you would not be able to either sit or shit for your lifetime.

P.S. I wouldn't mind butterscotch. ;) On the lightest note, how are you?

My love for her was growing leaps and bounds with every single word written by her that my eyes encountered. She had been there. It's just that I couldn't hear her, all throughout. Thanks to her dumbness. The other messages that followed went towards the serious note.

..... posted at 7.40 pm, 2nd September, 2008

Hey Jerk, where are you? Are you there? How come you have given up your net addiction so early? Are you a sanyasi or something? Do tell me because I've a bad news for you, I'm pregnant. Just kidding. Where the hell are you?

..... posted at 6.13 pm, 4th September, 2008

Jerk, are you even there? There have been no replies after your Shambhavi, Smriti and Dharawala mail. I've specially come for you to this irritating site, which no-one uses here in US. Have you been kidnapped?

..... posted at 8.32 am, 7th September, 2008

Is your net working, because, this networking is not-working? Wow, see that's what is called alliteration. Thank you, thank you. Your have made me a poet, my friend. Okay, tell me, are you constipated, having difficulty in speaking? :P

If it was for her, I wouldn't mind making noises even if I was constipated.

..... posted at 1.40 am, 7th September, 2008

WTH, dude, do you have any idea about how difficult it is for me to take time out. I've to lie about going to library and I've to stealthily go to a friend's place to use it. You don't know appreciation! GO TO HELL! ~!#$#%#

If I could reply to her scrap, I would have written, 'I'm already in hell.'

..... posted at 12.21 am, 10th September, 2008

Hey there? Why haven't you been responding? Are you really dating those three girls – oh what were their names – Shambhavi, Dhara and whoever that third bitch was? Though I seriously doubt that anyone would give you any'ghaas'! Not everyone is as foolish as me.

..... posted at 8.27 pm, 14th September, 2008

As expected, no replies from you. I even forgot my earlier email id and even yours. And you ain't any celebrity that I could find you on google. Why are you such an ass?

..... posted at 7.11 pm, 15th September, 2008

I've got news for you. I'm coming back. Contact the undersigned for more details. I bet you would.

The irritating dunce :P ;D
(ilovebutterscotch@gmail.com)

My excitement was soaring high. I could hear my heart thumping, in anticipation or fear, I don't know. Anticipation of seeing her once again, fear of encountering, rather being encountered by her mom.

….. posted at 7.11 pm, 17th September, 2008

Helloooooo, is there anybody alive out there? I feel like I'm talking to a wall.

Wait a minute, now you're going to talk to a wall. I'm never going to come again on this outdated social networking website. If by any chance, you happen to read this, be assured that I hate you more than anything else in this world. Now, to find me, you need to face the book! All my friends are there. I even tried searching Kanav Bajaj there, I found a couple of guys – none of them even a little bit close to your ugliness. They were uglier! See, I now even paid you a compliment. Adieu.

If love could be expressed as a mathematical function, it was the point of global maxima. Sorry for being nerdy, but at times, it makes me feel sexy. That's how nerds feel, in terms of sizes and curves, if you know what I mean.

I was happy. After all, she was happy, she was coming back and yes, she was supposedly in love with me, despite spending the past one month in the land of DiCaprio and Cruise. It's an achievement, if you happen to have a face like mine or if you happen to have had faced (critical situations) like me. I wanted to reply to each of her scraps, filling pages after pages pouring my heart out, thus finishing another novel.

There were no more replies after 17th September. As she had promised, she had moved to facebook. Facebook – that was not something in vogue in India in 2008. Avid Orkut users, who thought (some of them still think so!) that there could have been no better invention than Orkut to give their life a meaning – meaning to explore their stalking abilities, networking with like-minded individuals and dating the opposite sex, were strictly not willing to change.

In the year of 2007-08, I could bet that Orkut would have beaten the matrimonial websites such as Shaadi.com in terms of match-making. It was the lifeline for individuals like my earlier self, who experienced a full-throttle earthquake while talking to any girl. Since scrapping didn't require you to stand in front of a girl, trying to make an interesting conversation with your ass on fire, it made the whole process less painful.

I opened a new tab on my browser, typed the words facebook.com for the very first time in my life. Rather than trying to decipher how this new and suave social engine worked, I went to pursue something more important. As soon as I assimilated everything that I saw on the homepage, I didn't wait a moment to type her full name in the search box.

I waited anxiously. Facebook didn't understand my anxiety.

No results found for your query. Check your spelling or try another term.

I thought that I had been fooled by her or rather I misinterpreted her complicated face-my-book bullshit. I kept staring at the search results. When I looked for what I searched, I realized that I had indeed misspelt her name – Tanya Bajaj! I had already presumed her to be my wife. I corrected the name to Tanya Mehra – a dozen results fluttered in front of my eyes in a moment. Five of them had a profile picture of Kareena Kapoor, three of them of Katrina Kaif, one had my favourite – Priyanka Chopra's and the rest three had no profile pictures. I knew she had to be one amongst the last three. She is not so cheesy as to have a celebrity's picture as her profile picture – even though I have real feelings for Priyanka.

I clicked on the first profile. The profile info told me that Tanya Mehra belonged to Mysore. I chucked it. I went to the second one. The hometown was Delhi, I got thrilled. I steered through her profile. Her activities and interests included 'body piercings', 'Sexy After 30', 'Architects are sexy' and the most horrendous one 'Red nail-paint'. Her interests made me lose my interest in her. I moved to the third one.

I inwardly prayed to God for her to not be amongst those Katrinas and Kareenas. 'I would break up with her, no matter my excitement, if she happens to be one amongst those.' I said to myself.

The third and the most awaited profile opened. The wait was over.

Bio: Hi, I'm waiting. And that's not my name. ;)
Favorite Quotations: 'To inspire someone, love.'
Interests: Sarcasm. That's for you.
        Butterscotch. That's for me.
          Scrabble. That's for us.
Activities: Dreaming to get rid of the nightmare.
Address: Do you really want to come to my place?
Music: Chai chappa chai

That was the girl I'd been waiting for so long. My smile extended from one ear to another; had it extended a millimetre more my lips would have ruptured. Her privacy settings had been turned off and not only could I add her as a friend, but also poke her, which is one thing that I really wanted to do. Hearty thanks to Mark Zuckerberg for that! I messaged her –

Kanav Bajaj

So here you are. Why would you like to do a Chai chappa chai all alone?

Before I could go back to my homepage and wait for her reply, and make some new friends, my FB inbox showed one message. I liked facebook.

Tanya Mehra

Oh damn, you're alive! Who said I'm doing Chai chappa chai all alone, I am dating an American here. He's cute. :P

'Thank God, she isn't messaging herself here!' I screamed with joy.

The friend request was accepted in no time. She was online. What could have been a better surprise?

We were going to chat. We could have a full-fledged conversation, tease each other with words and other not-to-be-disclosed signs, poke each other and like each other – as many times as we wanted.

4.31 pm. 21ˢᵗ September, 2008

I: Hell-lo!

Tanya: I believe in giving, not taking.

I: I know. Nobody could testify that more than me. You gave me two months of loneliness, 27 nights with disturbed sleep, twenty two days of waiting to hear from you, three days with excessive mortification and one lonely night at a dilapilated bus-stand!

Tanya: That's one awesome love story! Come on, now thank me for all that.

I (stunned): Well, that's not true.

Tanya: Why not?

I literally fumbled while typing. I couldn't find a reason to say why not. I thought of telling her about my novel. It's hard to resist something that you've done from someone who was your inspiration to pursue the work. The dilemma of whether to give her a surprise later, if I get published, or unravel the novel through the boring medium of internet, perplexed me. I decided to wait in case a special opportunity may present itself in the future.

I (God forgive me for lying!): It was not at all awesome. I suffered all the while.

Tanya: What, what, what! You lustful jackass, you were the cause of all those sufferings, and you made me suffer through those things too. Couldn't you stop when I asked you to stop? Why did you have to go for one last kiss? You had 47 nights with disturbed sleep; I had exactly 54 nights – night from the very first day. Do you realize how one feels being alienated from one's own home-place, away from everything that you grew up with?

I: Aww, now don't get sentimental. I was just kidding. Our story is indeed awesome and funny too.

Tanya: Oh, I was just kidding. Now you've become senti. And do you know why our love story is awesome?

I (staring at the wall; facebook's wall): No.

Tanya: Oh dumbass! It's because I'm awesome.

I: And modest too.

Tanya: Well, that's god-gifted. On a serious note, how have you been?

I: Wrong question, to the wrong person, at the wrong time. Let me see, what could have possibly happened to make me unhappy? I lived a happy, contented life ever since you left me.

Tanya: I could see that. You ass, why didn't you answer my scraps on Orkut?

I: Ass. That's the word especially coined by Shakespeare for you. You bloody dumbass, do you know the level of your stupidity? All this while, you had been scrapping on your own scrapbook. You've become an American, literally after going to that land of dumbness.

Tanya: Are you serious?

I: Of course, yes!

Tanya: Oh shit! Why can't it be uncomplicated like facebook?

I: No.

Tanya: That's really embarrassing. But seriously, that social networking website sucks bigtime. I don't understand how you could tolerate it. The name itself sounds like 'chirkut'.

I: Funny.

Tanya: And I wondered what the hell happened to you.

I: Why wouldn't I have replied otherwise? I was stuck to my laptop for the last 14 days, 10 hours a day, if not more.

Tanya: For me? Were you waiting for my reply?

I: Oh ... (fumbling with typing)...yeah, with you, I mean, for you – your reply!

Tanya: *What? Don't tell me that you're such a girl. I mean 10 hours a day, awaiting my reply. WTH! Didn't you've any other work? I wish I hadn't come back. You're so idle!*

God forgive me that I expected stereotypical responses such as 'that's sweet' from her. Now that I was in the wrestling arena, I'd no option other than to fight.

I: *You're talking as if you didn't miss me at all.*

Tanya: *Of course not. I didn't miss you!*

I was heartbroken. She had entered some text; I was desperately waiting to throw my sympathy seeking tantrums, but waited for her to complete what she was writing first.

Tanya: *Now, I have got to go. It's already late. My mami is waiting.*

I: *Did you really not miss me?*

Tanya: *Yes, I didn't. You were by my side, all the time. Love isn't about physical presence, it's about emotional. Good night bubu, poochi! :* ;)*

I: *Bubu? What does that mean? Does it have to do anything with boobs? I like it if that's the case.:P*

Tanya is offline. <u>Send</u> *it as message instead.*

Abrupt ending, I didn't like that! I clicked on the send button, to make sure my vested interest in her was made clear to her.

Life couldn't have been happier. It seemed that my long wait had borne a fruit. The Orkut Tragedy seemed to be especially devised by the Master Craftsman to render my work possible. That day, I felt as if I was the richest person of this world.

I stared at the wall for the next five minutes, reading the entire chat three times over. I liked the name 'bubu', thinking it to be intricately linked to my 'grand' imagination. The content of our chat was totally useless. What mattered was the attachment. Each and every word that she had said to me was the best word that had ever struck my ears, sorry eyes. If I express it in an engineer's words, each word of hers was like a quantum of joy.

'That makes an awesome love story.' I echoed her words.

I jumped on my bed. Never before had the dust-laden ceiling fan above my head made me smile, cry and feel grateful simultaneously. There was a lizard on the wall, eyeing an ill-fated insect. I felt grateful even to that lizard. I wanted to thank it for its presence. I was in love, with everything in this universe. My eyes drifted. The cobwebs, which would have otherwise made me hysterical to *jhadoofy* them, helped in relaxing me beyond limit. I closed my eyes, to cut myself from what seemed like a dream-world to enter the blissful world of sleep.

'Wake up!' A loud shriek shattered all my bliss. My eyelashes which were glued to my eyes didn't like the sudden curtain-raising. I tried to see who was speaking so loudly. Unsurprisingly, Sameer, with his straight-from-the-belly baritone was the source of the magical voice – the voice closely resembled that of the Genie of the cartoon show

Arabian Nights. I was merely making sleepy noises like Alladin's monkey-friend Abu.

Sameer shook me by the shoulders and said excitedly. 'Dude, get up. You're missing the sight, I mean, you're missing the show of a lifetime.'

'What?' I said, puzzled.

'Come with me. Here's the thing.' Sameer dragged me near Aryan's door. There was already a conglomeration of idlers outside his room. 'Shhh. Listen to the noise coming from inside, I bet he's doing something wild.'

'I think he's sobbing.' I said, after eavesdropping carefully.

'Come on. Aryan and sobbing, that's like saying Anuj is in love.' Sameer remarked to everyone's amusement. He looked around for Anuj and seemed somewhat disappointed to find out that he wasn't around. Mockery is real only when the victim is standing close to the mocker.

'No, listen intently.' I said.

'Oh, "in-tent-lee"! Author-saab has already started showing off his vocab.' Sameer taunted. The victim, this time being near to the mocker, had no other option than to gleefully become a subject of the jeers of the mocker's accomplices.

But they did hear intently. And indeed, it was Aryan sobbing. When confirmed, I unbolted his door and entered the room along with the rescue-team. Aryan was in tears, holding something that seemed very familiar to me. WTF!

'Why are you crying, honey? Did Riya dump you?' Sameer said in the meanwhile, in a girl's voice.

'No, I read something that made me cry. It's Kanav's book.' Aryan said confidently, wiping his eyes.

'Did he write it so badly?' Shikhar, one of the uglier-than-me kinds, asked with a wicked smile.

I turned to Aryan, eagerly waiting for his reply. Was it really the case?

I stood there gaping. Aryan advanced towards me and said, 'Dude, you wrote an amazing book! This was the first fiction that I ever read and trust me when I say that I read it in one go, you even made me cry at the end. I've marked some places with pencil where language needs to be polished, but all in all, it is an excellent work.'

Amazed, I stood there, with my still sleepy eyes. 'This bliss is better than sleep.' I thought.

'So, when are you getting it published?' Aryan asked.

'Dude, are you kidding? Is it worth publishing?' I questioned, self-consciously.

'It's engrossing, with a good combination of humour and emotions in it. It would make a great light read. People like light reading nowadays.' Aryan said.

I cautiously analyzed each and every word of his and tried to trace any sign of sarcasm or mockery in his voice. It was not there. His sincerity showed through his face. It was pure delight.

I was flattered. I was delighted. And, I was confident. I wanted to share my delight with Tanya but there was another desire, that of surprising her with my published work. Desire preceded delight. I went along with it.

I went to finish my unfinished task. Sleep, my true love. The ceiling fan and the cobwebs didn't seem to be bothered by my ecstasy even a single bit. I liked them however, feeling more grateful to them than before. I was missing the divine presence of the little repugnant lizard, however. Besides, I was also missing the presence of that adorable social networking wizard, on the facebook wall. The thought swayed from wall to wall, until it thought of sitting in the back seat of my mind.

I had a dream. I dreamt of holding my published novel in my hand and handing it over to Tanya, teasing her by saying, 'This one's for you. If it hadn't been your absence, I would never have been able to complete this.'

I got up, all of a sudden, without any Genie from the Arabian Nights. I was inspired, by the dream to dream. I wanted to get published, so desperately that I would have given up my studies for its sake. By the way, giving up studies is no big deal.

At 2 o' clock at night, I sat down and googled publishers, read the blogs of authors and got discouraged at every single moment. One recently published author wrote – don't expect much until your last name sounds like Bhagat or Rushdie. I didn't want to go for an affidavit just for the sake of publishing, so I started writing to publishers.

Within one hour, I mailed around a dozen publishers giving them a brief synopsis of my work and anxiously waited for their reply. I certainly knew that no publisher in India would be online at that moment of time, but I also knew that no such truth was going to suppress my anxiety.

I opened my blog and penned down a note on passion:

My Passion

Someone asked me, 'What is success, in your eyes?'

'Success is finding your passion', I replied.

'What is passion?' He asked.

'It is anything which can make you lose your sleep.'

'Have you ever lost it?' He enquired.

I opened my eyes and exclaimed, 'I did!'

And I began writing this.

I've found my passion, and you?

Love made me realize my passion. Or rather loss of love. Suddenly, my FB chat window popped up with the noise of uncorking of champagne.

Sent at 5.35 pm

Tanya: Yes, it's inspired from boobs. Do you want them?

I: Oh…damn! It was you. I was scared.

Tanya: Who're you sleeping with? Jackass!

I: Nothing, it's just google. By the way, I do want boobs.

Tanya: Boring, you're! I thought you would've found them in the last one month.

I: Nah, my bad luck is so good that I don't have a chance of getting laid in the near future. However, I found something else equally enchanting during the last one month.

Tanya: And what's that – one man orchestra? ;)

I: Yes. Indeed. It's fun, you know.

I joked. One man orchestra had been a discovery of my school days – long showers and extreme constipation often being the most-used alibi.

Tanya: Lucky you. I didn't even get a chance.

I: Why do you need a chance? You have already got those heavy baskets of joy to play around with?

Tanya: Okay, Bubu, that's too much for the night for you to play your orchestra with. Now tell me, what did you find?

I: My love. My passion. I found the thing that could make me lose my sleep.

Tanya: That's sweet. I know I'm so hot. Now come on, I've got just 5 mins. Tell me how have you been?

She didn't seem interested in my latest find. And yes, I had so many questions to ask her.

I: Since I'm alive and can chat, you already know that I'd been able to carry myself through everything. Where are you? How had you been all the while?

Tanya: Finally, I get the question that I'd been waiting for a long time. Now, since you've asked – it's going to be me, who'll be speaking for the next 5 minutes. Just listen, don't interrupt.

I: Ok!

Tanya: I said don't interrupt, you jerk!

I: Ok, I won't. :P

Tanya: Huh! So, we got screwed up on 27th, right?

I: Unscrewed up, actually! :P

Tanya: Very funny. So, we were caught on 27th. I ran back into my house when you were caught, fearing that once done with the fatal interaction with my Mom, you would again ask me for a final kiss, since I lost that bet and therefore you would have had both of us killed.

I: Totally!

Tanya: On a serious note, I went into the house. Once done with the drama and action, my mother raced in and she didn't say a word. She went to my room and took out all of my books, gift-items and other 'inexpensive' things, and rushed towards the kitchen. I ran after her, snatching everything from her hand, crying when she shrieked, 'You don't need any of this. You've turned every expectation of mine into ashes. You don't deserve to stay here; I'm sending you to Paritosh's place in US.' Paritosh is my mama's name – equally conservative and thousand times more ferocious.

I cried, 'No, Ma! Please, you can't do this to me.' I was sobbing uncontrollably.

She said, 'I've no other choice.'

I screamed, 'I'll die if you do that.'

She had no mercy. I had killed every hope of hers. She was outraged. After two minutes of awkward pause, she said suddenly, 'If you promise me that you would never meet that bastard again, I'll let you stay here. And, trust me when I say that you would have to walk over my dead body if you ever break the promise.'

I was at my wit's end. She left me no choice. Coming out of my subdued shell for the first time in my life, I dared to utter, 'I love Kanav. Send me wherever you want, I'm gonna be with him for the rest of my life.'

I: Wow, that's ... cute, yes that's the word. :D

Tanya: She gave me one tight slap on the cheek and started beating me with both her hands.

I: like a dholak?

Tanya: Yes, you sadist! I didn't cry then, neither did I revolt. She stopped beating me when I didn't reciprocate at all. Once she had taken out her anger on me, there was no reason to be scared. But all the same, I was very worried. I didn't want to rebel anymore, since she is a heart patient. Her ears had turned red and her breathing became erratic. Her blood pressure had shot up, as could be seen from the rage in her eyes. I went to her, held her hand and asked, 'are you still angry?'

I: Didn't she resume her dholak concert once again?

Tanya: No. She just left. When anger doesn't work, resentment does. She didn't talk to me for two whole days. She took my cellphone, she removed the mouse and keyboard from the computer – being non-technical, she couldn't find a better way and she sat near the landline, to monitor any call that came. I had no options other *than seeing her do these things. It was during that time that you called and got a wholesome ass-kicking. I was sitting in the same room as the telephone, when your call came. I almost burst out laughing when she caught you. I could not say anything to her. Her silence did the trick, I couldn't say a thing.*

I: You could have just farted.

Tanya: Not funny. I said no interruption.

I: Fart is no interruption. It can be silent.

Tanya: Stop it. You're full of shit.

I: No, I'm full of fart.

Tanya: Are you interested in hearing me out?

I: Yes yes, sorry. Continue.

Tanya: So, there I was trapped in that little house. My mom didn't say anything in the two days that followed, and neither did I. When she used to go outside, she used to take the telephone with her and lock me inside. I had no idea what she was up to until two days later. Two days later I hear that I was going to US, to Paritosh's place.

I: You call your Mama by his name?

Tanya: He's such a scary person that you would have called him with ill-names. At least, my way of disrespecting is casual.

I: Wait a minute. What's he like?

Tanya: He's like someone you would never like. A strict disciplinarian – gets up at 4 o' clock in the morning, takes a cold water bath, goes for a 10 mile run and wants a breakfast at 7, with five newspapers and 3 coffees. His wife, my mami is another sample. She does everything an hour before her husband and believe me when I say that she is the boss. Both are ultra-conservative, short-tempered and sick.

I: OMG. Your family is full of buffoons. Have those clowns got any baby-clown?

Tanya: *Shut up. They've a daughter, aged 5 – Divya. She's cute. Speaks like an American. Here's a story for you. Once she came from her school and asked my Mami, 'What's sex, Mamma?' My mami got so angry that she rubbed her teeth with red chilly, screaming at her never to say that word again. I was horrified.*

I: Poor child! She could have just said that it's another word for gender.

Tanya: *That's what! When Divya got back to her senses, she came with a piece of paper and pointed her finger at it. It was a painting competition form where she had to fill her name, sex and school. Hey Bubu, I got to go now. My angry-young-mama would freak out otherwise.*

I: When would you come back? Any phone number.

Tanya: *No fixed time. Screw you if you ask for phone number once again. Bye.*

I: Phone number? Now, you can commit the divine task that I'd been waiting for since a long time… ;)

Tanya Mehra is offline. <u>Send</u> it as a message instead.

Abrupt ending – so typical of her. Everything went around without much crackling noise or news for the next couple of weeks. Tanya used to come online once in a while, when I used to have those little moments of joy talking to her. Her Hitler like maternal uncle and his wife did no good to her frustration and she would often complain about some thing that her irascible mami had said to her, which in turn irritated me. Her condition was worse than that in India, with her Mom. Though she had the access to everything to contact me, she was constantly being monitored, when at home. Her Paritosh mamu was so particular about every other thing that he scanned all her phone-bills – each and every number she used, web-browsing history etc.

One day, she brought some news for me. She had got into a college – Smith College, of Northampton. Massachusetts. Other than the fact that it was a Women's college, its other unique value propositions were its notable alumni such as the then first lady of US, Barbara Bush and former first lady, Nancy Reagan. That brightened my chances of being able to pee in the Air Force One someday, if I managed to escape the traps of her cannibalistic family after marrying her.

Meanwhile, publishers seemed to have gone into hibernation – the dream of getting published seemed to be an over-ambitious leap of my imagination. I just prayed to my eternal enemy not to make me go for an affidavit. I suddenly felt so incompetent about the fact that I couldn't even share the fact with Tanya that I wrote a book on us while she was away.

Meanwhile, according to the suggestion of my dear local management guru Sri Sri Sameer Shankar, I started applying for summer internships, targeting Massachusetts as my primary destination. The classes had been so hectic with such nasty professors, who would first drive us to sleep and then scold us for sleeping, that at the end of the day most of us would either be left idling or debating on issues ranging from philosophy, science, business, to the ultimate topic – pornography. Aryan even proposed a super-sexy business model for the 3-D porn business in India.

Once during the class, we were laughing at some random jokes. Our professor, whose baldness spoke volumes about his erudition, got psyched with our insolence. He came towards us and asked each one of us to stand up.

We rose from our seats, quite delighted with the sudden recognition and faced the blackboard in the attention position, waiting for the anthem to start. It started, in the same placid and monotonous tone, which every professor on this planet is endowed with since his geeky childhood.

'Come on, share the joke with me. I'm also interested in having fun.' The pedagogue was at his best sarcastic mood. He liked mortifying students.

None of us replied. How could we? It's not advisable to utter words during the anthem, you know.

'Come on, tell me.' He reprimanded.

'One should always respect teachers – they're the ones who make you dream. This was what we were talking about, Sir.' Aryan said, stooping to hide the obvious smile from the bald devil.

There erupted a silent laughter across the classroom. Aryan had played a gimmick, which was well-understood by the fellow students. The professor stood there, bewildered.

We were trying to suppress our laughter, by turning our heads here and there. Finally, all of us looked down at our very dear desks, but looking at the rude inscriptions drawn there by our horny alumni did no good to stop our laughter.

'Well, that's indeed funny. Ass... you find it.' The professor did not allow the slip-of-the-tongue to take place. We missed it.

He went back to the blackboard. We sat down.

'Ah, I forgot to ask you people something.' He said.

'Yes sir.' Sameer said, obsequiously.

'Get out of the class. All of you.' He said with a shrewd smile. His smooth head shone in sadistic ecstasy.

We left one by one. The whole class jeered at us by making faces or passing rude remarks. We appreciated the jealousy; after all we got respite from the boring lecture.

It was after a long time that all four of us were together, attending the same class – now chucked out of the same class. It being an evening class, was the primary reason for our attendance – no sleep-deprivation, no morning dates made the impossible possible. Anuj, with his constipated face seemed to be robbed of happiness.

'What happened? Why so serious?' Sameer asked Anuj.

'I was peeping into the cell-phone of Anusha, the girl who was sitting in front of me – I was reading the SMSes that she was typing to her boyfriend. It was so scandalizing. You guys spoilt my moment of joy.'

'What was she typing? Tell me?' Sameer asked, curiosity dripping from his eyes.

'She wrote – "you remember last night, we were all alone at your place and suddenly you"…' Anuj began and paused, all of a sudden.

'Yes, what happened next?' Sameer stammered, in excitement.

'Ah! Good things don't come so easy. Treat me with two muffins to know what's next.'

'Rascal! I won't get you two muffins. Your story will not be worth two muffins.'

'You bet. It's worth a thousand muffins.'

'Oh really? I'll treat to you another. That makes two.' Aryan said, getting interested all of a sudden despite his unconcerned self.

'First treat me, only then I will tell.' Anuj persisted.

The duo gave in and treated him with two chocolate muffins. I was happy since I managed to scoop out a bite from one of them.

'Now tell us the story!' Sameer said. He was already getting impatient, with his fingers making abrupt movements around his body and his head wobbling on his neck, as if his bones were made of springs.

'Oh yes, the story…is that…' Anuj said, in pauses, 'Anusha wrote, "you remember last night, we were all alone at your place and suddenly you discovered this new way to extract two muffins from your dumb friends." Thanks for the muffin, by the way.' Anuj said and ran away from us and disappeared in the library.

'Asshole!' Aryan shouted at the top of his voice, making three professors turn their moon-top towards him in disgust.

'See! They realized that I was calling them.' Aryan said, indicating the professors to us. We couldn't agree more.

I went back to my hostel and unable to find Anuj for an ass-kicking, I decided to let my sagging body rest. I dozed off. I got up at 3.30 am, with a strange lull and gruesome darkness around me. I didn't know what had suddenly happened. After wrestling with my amnesia for two minutes, I could finally make out that I was in the same world that I left before I dozed off.

By habit, I checked my mail and all – there was nothing new. Tanya, due to her tedious college schedule, wasn't all that active on the social network, for the past few days. Neither did I possess anything else to soothe my depressed state of mind. It was me, my unpublished manuscript and my tireless hope to receive a reply from a publisher, to accompany me in my lonely room.

Bored of loitering around the World Wide Web, with no special threads to trap me, I moved out. The light was on in Anuj's room. I decided to be his guest for sometime. He always had some raunchy stories to tell. His experience had by now outshone that of his guru – Aryan. And he was not at all shy about talking about anything – be it his personal life or his ex's.

I knocked, making a very faint noise. He took some time to open the door.

'What the hell are you doing at 4 o' clock in the morning?' Anuj said, smoking a Marlboro.

'I was getting bored. Thought of disturbing you.'

'Come in. Want a puff?' He asked, generously.

'No thanks! You're asking the wrong person.' I said.

'*Sati-savitri* saala!' He remarked. I didn't pay attention, though it sounded cute, in a weird way.

'You know what? Smokers inspire me.'

'Oh really? How?'

'They inspire me not to try smoking.'

'I saw a slapstick remark coming. I smoke just 5 cigarettes a day. That's nothing if you compare it to Manas, who is not satisfied with less than 20.' He said, dragging a mouthful of nicotine inside. I could visualise his black-washed lungs, which would be serving as *kajal* for lady bacteria inside his wind pipe.

'Nice role models, you have. Anyhow, tell me something interesting. Something entertaining. I'm completely bored.'

'Ummm…I can't think of anything interesting as of now.' Thankfully, his cigarette ended with the next puff. Now it was I, him and the residual smoke in the room, which wasn't as suffocating as the fresh one.

'Okay, tell me have you ever cheated on your girlfriends?'

'Hmmm…' Anuj contemplated, and said, 'well, I've never actually cheated on my girlfriends. But, yes, I got molested by a lot of other girls during my relationships.'

Soon a wink followed. I realized the level of his expertise. Awesome, indeed.

'Nice. You're on the right track, with a lot of wrong girls. What more could you want?'

'What about you? You must be the same *sati-savitri* of all time?'

'Yes, I'm committed to the one and only.'

'What base have you conquered till date?'

'Base? I don't understand.' I said, in all innocence.

'Come on dude! Now don't tell me that you don't know what base is. Base is…I mean…so basic. You learn it before you learn LOGO in school.'

'I have been dumb since my childhood. Now, will you please tell me?'

'Gosh! You're such an ass. Dude, you don't know what base is – I mean you've a girlfriend sucker, you don't know. Oh my f-god, I can't believe it.'

'Don't believe it. And don't tell me also. Keep on shouting your "Oh my Gods" a million times more until your God comes down here to take you with him.' I yelled angrily.

'Base is the level of intimacy. Base 1 is smooch. Base 2 is embracing, squeezing and getting intimate. Base 3 is the play of hand. Base 4 is you know what!' He said, shyly.

'Oh I already knew that. I just wanted to see that discomfort in your voice, while saying that. Even your vast experience couldn't remove that shyness of yours. *Ladki!*

Ah, that sweet flavour of mockery. How good does it feel! His patronizing attitude a moment earlier was buried somewhere deep inside his serious face. He was blank –reflective – must have been thinking about how to come up with a reply to my ego-killing mockery. I felt the need to chill him a bit, to encourage him a bit, to flatter him a bit and I did exactly that.

'So Mr. Thinker, what base have you conquered till date?' I said, hoping that this would embark him on his conceited boat of tales, containing innumerable experiences with the fairer sex.

'Don't remind me of that. It was one of worst nightmares in my life.'

'What?'

'Dude, there couldn't be a worst tragedy than this one. I could beat Shakespeare if I knew literature and penned it down.'

'What is that?'

'You know Block VI?'

'Yes, of course. That isolated block where our boring Atmospheric Studies classes are held.'

'Yes. I went there with my second girlfriend Niki at half past 2. I had spent 10 hours in convincing her about the block and its inactivity at night.'

'A guard caught you two?' I asked, shooting wild guesses.

'No. It would have been much better if someone had caught us. We were really desperate to do it. Niki is the awesomest girl I've ever met. I mean, she is one of those kinds who one would never want to leave. "Perfect" in everything – I hope you get what I mean.'

'Yaya, I get it. So what was it?'

'I was fully prepared to do it. And so was she. We went to the ladies loo first, but it was too small, so we decided to try out gents' washroom. At 2, there's nobody around – so we thought it would be equally good – plus more spacious too.'

'Okay…!' I was assimilating everything that was being said, enraptured after a long time.

'We went inside, bolted the door from inside. We started off as soon as we faced each other. It was wild. It was violent. It was crazy. I didn't even realize how bases 1 and 2 were conquered as soon as we began and I was just going to crack base 3 when she pushed me away.'

His description was racy; I could see from his eyes that whatever he said was the exact truth. My eagerness killed my patience and I screamed, 'What happened next!'

'She was facing the washroom's door. Her face was shell-shocked!

She exclaimed, "OMG! That's Niti's phone number written on the door. And that's your handwriting, isn't it?" I looked at the door. I didn't realize that it was the loo that carried all my graffiti.'

'What the heck! Are you kidding me?'

'Dude, I had such a mortifying break-up with Niti – she had caught me red-handed dating her roommate Niki, the very same girl. I was cheating on her. Humiliated, I came back to college and bunked my classes and jerked off in that particular loo, letting my frustration on the door.'

'That's ridiculous. Get away.' I said in disgust.

'What's ridiculous? Shagging – just because you're a bloody eunuch!' Anuj shouted.

'Yes. What happened next?'

'I accepted my defeat. She went outside the loo while I, having nothing better to do, played solo.'

'And don't tell me that the door was once again made into your phonebook.'

'No.' Anuj said.

'Thankfully.' I sighed.

'Oh that's because I didn't have a pen that time.'

'Asshole.' I swore and made a rapid exit from his room. I was disgusted. Not by his rabid sexual encounters, but by his insensitivity. Though, the inward desire to visit the same washroom to get a glimpse of the alphanumeric graffiti, painted my imagination all throughout.

Men, you know, are dogs by default.

Contemplative, I returned to my room. The lull that prevailed earlier was encroached by the sudden chirping of birds, which seemed excited while flying across the newly lit sky. My tinted windows beheld a sight of an unnatural natural beauty. It was one of the first times in my college life that I saw a sunrise.

I felt hopeful. I felt good. And, I felt free – from negativities. And, perhaps for the first time in my life, I went for an early morning bath. I bathed in cold water; the cold drops when kissed my body made me feel – no, it's not awesome, it's not rejuvenated, it's not amazing and neither it is blissful. It made me frigging frozen. Each and every drop was like a sharp needle pricking against my soft skin. Was I bloody out of my mind to take a cold water bath on an early October morning? The early morning bliss was ruthlessly butchered by my stupidity. I ran back to my room, trembling apace, dropping off my towel on the way – thankfully no one was awake to catch hold of my cute ass.

It took me nine minutes of sitting underneath a blanket to come back to life. Nine – the magic number of life-creation, isn't it? I decided to test my luck on that eventful day. I had a feeling that I was to receive a reply from the publishers. I logged in my mailbox.

There was just one mail. It was not from my publishers. It was from the lady from Northampton.

Dear Bubu,

Paritosh caught me going to my friend's place to surf the net. I'm no more allowed to do that. He has hired a spy driver to keep a track on my activities. It seems that their only purpose in this life is to screw up my life. I'm feeling so suffocated. I want to run away from this place.

I even tried to scare my Mom by telling her that I would commit suicide if they keep on caging me anymore. She said go ahead, since I was already dead for her. I don't know what to do. I won't be able to access internet from now on, until I find another way out. Don't worry about me. I'm not going to allow them to be the cause of my sorrow. I'm going to fight and I'm going to accomplish something, to stop being dependent on them.

I love you. And I miss you. God has given us enough sorrow, he'd better get us some happiness otherwise we will snatch it.

Love.

Tanya

P.S. This is Shelly – Tanya's college-mate. She asked me to send this message to you.

Life is not always easy when your loved one comes back. I never felt so cold inside. My feet felt numb. I wanted to throw my laptop out of the window. That could give you an idea about the extent up to which I hated that moment.

When your heartbeat is on the internet, you can't plug the wire off. I didn't reply. I did not want to wait for her reply anymore. I was cursing my luck for having fallen for a girl, with such a diseased family. Or rather, for having a girl, from such a diseased family, fall for me. I looked left, towards the mirror. I looked devastated – so much that nobody would have believed that I've had a cold water bath early in the morning.

My eternal enemy seemed to be back from His hibernation. He couldn't stand seeing me happy. In rage, I took out a blank sheet from my notebook and wrote –

GOD, you know what? You Suck Bigtime!

I stapled that slogan on the bulletin board in front of my table, so that whenever my eyes drifted from making love to my girlfriend, it could convey my hatred to the Almighty. I felt somewhat better. I decided that I should reply to Shelly. But before that, I decided to check her out on facebook. Men are dogs, I already told you. We need just a small reason – girls – to come out of any psychic trouble, emotional dilemma or sentimental tornado.

I checked her out. She was cute. As I'm such a decent guy, being already taken, I would not like to describe her using raunchy adjectives such as well-endowed, big, hot or ravishing, which perfectly fitted her persona.

I went back to reply to Shelly, charming her with my newly found writer self. However something prevented me from doing the flirtation. That was the new mail in my inbox. The subject was gratifying enough to postpone the wanton flirting by sometime.

Subject: A token of appreciation

Dear Kanav,

It has been a pleasure receiving the manuscript of your novel 'Kismat Disconnection'. Our editorial team went through the entire work and would like to acknowledge you for the fact that you've written a riveting story at such a young age. However, since the story seemed to have an extra dose of imagination, it could not fit in the realistic fiction domain that we publish. We mean to say that the reader would never be convinced with the climax of the book – where braces get entangled with the girl's lips. This scene seemed to be too unrealistic.

We would advise you to re-write your manuscript, with more emphasis on making the storyline realistic so that readers can easily relate to it while reading your work. Also, the title seems too filmy, which needs to be changed.

We look forward to hear from you.
Regards,
Shailesh Deva
Chief Editor
Pingu India

I was stunned. Without wasting another moment, I took out another plain sheet and wrote with a marker – WTF! Somebody tell him that I had been through each and every situation that was described there. I was absolutely disappointed. I read the letter once again. The 'Deva' part of the editor's name seemed scary. It reminded me of the real 'deva', who sucks, as was being said by the slogan on my bulletin board.

Still, since he sounded interested, I decided to give it a go. Forgetting the flat belly of the American Shelly, I concentrated my entire energy on connecting kismat through my Kismat Disconnection.

I edited the climax completely, made it completely fake – so-called realistic in their terms. I did not love writing it. I did not live what I wrote. I did not have any feelings attached to it. It turned out to be irritating, boring and draggy. In one day, I mailed them back the result of my monotony, expecting a quick reply from them.

A day followed. My wait grew endlessly. Meanwhile, I did reply to Shelly –

Dear Shelly,

Thank you so much. We are going through a very tough time, I am grateful to God that He has provided us with such nice friends like you. By the way, what do you do?

Best

Kanav

Another publisher seemed to have arisen from his slumber as I received another mail that afternoon itself.

Dear Mr. Kanav,

Thanks for your manuscript. We liked it. We would like to publish it, but for that you would need to come to our office for signing the agreement. Would tomorrow be fine with you?

Regards,

Shyam Das

Carpet Fallings India
M-32, Connaught Place
New Delhi
+91-99583xxxxx

Excited, I called Mr. Das instantly to inquire about the timings. The conversation turned out to be heartening.

'Hello, is it Mr. Das?'

'Yes.'

'Hello Sir, this is Kanav, author of Kismat Disconnection.'

'Oh right son, great to hear from you. How are you?'

'I'm fine sir. Well, when can I come to meet you?'

'Oh right now, if you wish.'

'Well, I'm on my way sir.'

'We will keep the agreement prepared.'

I got dressed up, as well as I could. The memories of my first date came flooding in my mind. Upon speculation, I realized that once again, I had to take the metro – the same metro that paved way to the poignant disaster last time. I thought of taking Aryan along; signing an agreement seemed to be a tricky business for a person illiterate about legality. Aryan eagerly volunteered to come along. Eagerness owing to the fact that he could meet his dear Riya once we got free.

I was excited, so much so that I did not even bother to 'check out' the crowd aboard. Much like the last time, the thrill was anticipatory.

I just hoped not to get assaulted with any more oops in my life. Aryan was busy typing elaborate messages to his beloved, with his blackberry while his head was making the pose of Rodin' sculpture – The Thinker.

Bored, I decided to look down at my cell screen but unfortunately the two previous months had been a recession period for my cell phone. No messages, no regular rings and nothing to expect made my cell phone a morbid part of my life. What once used to be my lifeline was now no more than a mere mechanical device which occasionally vibrated – to nobody's use, occasionally quivered to life and occasionally displayed some random smileys. The earlier SMSes, some of them carrying the spark of my once newly sprouted love life, seemed to be belonging to an extremely distant past, somewhere in a vaguely different world. The mobile, as they called it, became an immobile part of my stagnant life.

A sudden jerk on the metro brought me back to life, when a voice of deep baritone helped us know, 'Rajiv Chowk Station. Please mind the gap.'

After strolling through the likes of Nizam's, PVR Plaza and the colourful circumference of the Connaught circus, we located the office of Carpet Fallings India. We were greeted by a very benevolent lady, who benignly asked us to be seated.

I looked around. There were three doors on the three sides, with flashy name-plates stuck to them mentioning Conference hall, Chief Editor and Pantry. There was a small door near one of the corners, which didn't say a thing but had a poster stuck to it – with a slogan

'Do not disturb – On an urgent call!' with the clip art of a toilet seat on it.

I liked the ambience, and so did Aryan. There was a bulletin board on the right side of the room which contained the cover page of all the novels published by the house. Some of them were quite popular. I was dazed, already imagining me to be a part of the world of authors – adorned with fame, recognition and money.

'Hello, Mr. Bajaj. I am Shyam Das, the chief editor.' A voice boomed from near the door. A suave gentleman in deep blue suit came forward with a slightly fake smile on his face. He looked old, knowledgeable and experienced. The meeting was not a meeting, but rather a massage – ego-massage, but not for me.

As I moved forward to shake my hand, he extended his hand to Aryan.

'So, Mr. Bajaj, how have you been?' He said.

Aryan looked stunned, while I, embarrassed, was suddenly submerged in the deep algal sea called inferiority complex.

'Meet Kanav Bajaj.' Aryan passed over the old 'baton' to me.

'Oh! I'm sorry. I presumed this handsome young man to be Kanav. Your good name please?' Mr. Das' eyes were on Aryan, all throughout.

'No problem. I'm Aryan.' Aryan said.

Once again, Mr. Das decided to shake hands with the 'handsome young man'.

'So, Mr. Bajaj. We went through your work. It was good. How did you find it, Mr. Aryan?' Mr. Das said, seemed to be unusually inclined towards Aryan.

'It's pretty good.'

'Yes, that's what made us consider the manuscript. We generally do not consider debutante authors but we really liked your work. Even Mr. Aryan found it pretty good.' His words seemed sarcastic.

'Do you also write Mr. Aryan?' Mr. Das hit the bull's eye.

'No, I just read.' Aryan said, humbly.

'What do you like reading?' Mr. Das pursued his bizarre interest in my former roommate with delight. Aryan looked at me, in desperate vexation.

'I like reading minds. And frankly speaking, I do not like yours.' Aryan said bluntly.

The sudden setback to Mr. Das's advancement towards the 'hot' property in his office didn't hinder the gaiety (read: gay-ty) of his spirits.

'So, where is the agreement? I would like to have a look.' I uttered to change the topic of our discussion to the actual topic of our discussion.

'Sure, here it is. You're just a signature away.' Mr. Das handed over the agreement to me. Thankfully, he didn't hand it to the man of his interest.

Aryan and I went through the agreement minutely. Upon close inspection, a clause stood out and captured our curiosity. It said:

The AUTHOR has to pay the PUBLISHER a fixed sum of money per copy for the first 10,000 copies of the book. This is to ensure that the publisher's initial expenses are covered up. If the AUTHOR fails to pay the required amount, the PUBLISHER is not obligated to give him/her any royalty.

We felt something fishy. The idea of paying the publishers sounded okay but for 10,000 copies seemed too much.

'Sir, what's the exact sum of money per copy that needs to be paid for the first 10,000 copies?'

'Oh, it's just the formality. The amount for debut authors is like 50 rupees per book. That makes one time lump sum of just five lacs rupees.'

'That's "just" five lacs rupees.' Aryan said to me, with a cunning smile on his face.

'And what's the royalty?' I asked the Mr. Das.

'For the first 5000 copies, you won't get any. For the further copies, it would be around 20 rupees per book.' Mr. Das said placidly.

'So, why don't you sign the agreement?' Mr. Das handed over a fountain pen to me.

'Sir, I'm just a student. How would I pay the required amount?'

'You should have thought about that before writing the book. Don't worry, it will be managed.' Mr. Das said, brutally.

'Mr. Aryan, why don't you try convincing Mr. Bajaj to sign the agreement?'

Aryan looked at me and winked. His face foretold me about what was going to come ahead.

'Kanav, why don't you sign the agreement? Come on, what are

you thinking? You would never get an opportunity like this ever again. Here's the pen, come on sign it.'

I didn't reciprocate, simultaneously looking at Mr. Das. He looked contented with a little sign of eagerness on his face.

'Come on, why don't you sign it? We'll manage the money. Oh come on, you dumbass, what the hell are you waiting for? Take the pen and sign the damn thing!' Aryan yelled.

I took the pen and decided to give it a go. I poured down my emotions in my signature and handed over the agreement to Aryan to see whether he was satisfied or not. He looked proud of me. We gathered our stuff for a swift exit and Aryan passed on the file to Mr. Das, 'Here you go Mr. Das. It's something that you required so badly.'

Mr. Das opened the agreement and what he beheld made him literally pee in his shiny pants. We both shouted, 'In thy face, Das saheb,' intentionally extending our 'ring finger' at him, just in courtesy.

My signature contained nothing but a simple graffiti: ,!,,

We went out and Aryan gave me a wholesome dose.

'Dude, I'm never going to come along with you ever again. Whenever I hang out with you, I encounter a disoriented character.' Aryan chided me.

'Oh, you're talking as if you didn't have fun. Come on, you can't deny the awesome fun that we had.'

'Oh I had fun.' Aryan moved forward his fist and pulled out the ring finger slowly and shouted, 'In thy face, Das saheb.'

'Did we do the right thing? Shouldn't we have bargained?'

'Did you really want to be a crushed mosquito beneath that loser?'

I was dumbstruck. I negated his direct question, not by logic but by fear.

'Don't be scared. You're good. You deserve a good publisher.'

'Thanks.' I mumbled, trying to assimilate the sudden hike in my self-esteem.

I gave Aryan a wholesome treat at Nizam's as a token of my gratitude for his moral support. My decision to take him with me turned fruitful.

One by one, rejections came. Some didn't like my non-writer profile, some had problems with my age, some had problems with a love story, some had a problem with my writing style, some had a problem with my life's true story – they said that it seemed too imaginative. If I could change the meaning of the word disappointment in the dictionary, I would have described my state during that time there. Even after submitting a modified manuscript to Pingu India, they seemed to have gone into hibernation and despite my persistent mails to them they didn't reply.

I was totally hopeless, once again. My girlfriend had been kidnapped and taken to the other side of the world; the side of the world where I belonged had nothing for me. It seemed that Tanya had taken away all my happiness along with her. The title 'Kismat Disconnection' used to mock me by reminding that indeed my fate had been tossed upside down.

Almost daily, I used to write in my diary, lines to my beloved telling her whatever happened to me. But alas! I couldn't send her my long articulate full-of-no-shorthands drafts. Damn the idea of the novel as a surprise!

11th November, 2008

Dear Bubu,

I wish I could tell you the struggle that I'm facing right now. Every day begins in hope and ends in disappointment. The feeling of hopelessness has crawled into each and every vein of my body. Yes, I'm sounding literary. After all, I'm a writer. No, don't think that I'm being fake. Okay, I won't sound so if you wish. But seriously, struggle has to have its limit. Nobody is willing to publish our love story - is it so boring? Are you so unappealing? Wait a minute, I know what you're going to say. No, it's not my character in my book that's repelling the publishers. Come on, I'm not so bad. If I had been, tell me would you have ever fallen in love with me?

I wish I could share with you the fact that I have penned down our love story, I spent my days and nights writing our very own story, and the way it has turned out, I want to share each and every feeling that passed through my soul while writing it. Not that it has turned out to be a literary masterpiece, but it has made my wait for you an unforgettable part of my life since it made me come face-to-face with my passion. It was as if you sat beside me and laughed and played with my imagination all throughout as I relished putting down those words and weaving the story. Again, I think I'm getting dragged to the writer's self. I want to be me more now, since you love me, not a stranger who writes love stories. But I also know that you would start loving that stranger once you read his book.

Lost in your love,
Struggling writer

Another self-dominated diary entry got trapped between the heavy bundles of pages above it. There weren't many pages left below to fight back the burden above. The page, carrying the helpless scribble of a struggling artist, succumbed to the weight and got immersed in gruesome darkness. The darkness that needed another sunrise of hope to conquer it.

The morning sun kept losing the brightness of hope. Tanya kept playing hide and seek with me while her friend Shelley intimated me frequently about her whereabouts. She was fine, doing good and busy in catching up with her studies. The worst reality of life: even pretty girls need to study. She was enjoying the 'Amriki' culture and at the same time, she had somehow adjusted with her maternal family. Once in a while, Shelley used to write to me talking about Tanya's longing. Her one mail made my heart melt:

15th November

Heya Kanav,

It's Shelley this side. I'm not supposed to tell you but I can't resist: Tanya has been missing you like crazy and it has been a long time now. She portrays herself to be strong but she isn't. She has been doing so many things for you that your entire mailbox can't hold its weight.

I just wish you two meet as soon as possible otherwise she would kill everyone here in US and run back to India. She's damn crazy about you! Alas, are you really that good as she says? Because I find your FB pic quite wicked.

Best
Shelley

So there was a flip-side to my beloved's humorous self - she was hiding her pain. Generally, I love surprises, but that time I felt choked. Her wet eyes appeared before my eyes and didn't go away, despite my numerous attempts to get rid of them. Her image clung to my vision and didn't vanish until my eyes turned wet themselves. I realized why committed people always want to be single. Love hurts.

It was four days to Tanya's birthday, 19th November, and the only thing that I wanted was to talk to her face to face. I couldn't fight that sinking feeling of guilt, pain and loneliness anymore. I wanted us to share our sentiments instead of holding them back. I wrote back to Shelley.

Dear Shelley,

Thanks for writing to me. I would be really grateful if you could arrange a video chat on her birthday. This wicked guy needs to speak to her and surprise her.

Regards,
Kanav

I didn't know what to say but I did know that I had a lot to say. I waited.

On 18th November, an interesting thing happened. I received an unexpected mail from a publishing house called Eucalyptus Publishing House, to which I hadn't written. The mail said that they were new publishers and they had heard about my book from my college-mates. I googled the publishing house, but even google didn't give any hint about the existence of any such publication house. I was confused. I mailed him the synopsis and two chapters of my book, which he had asked for, suspiciously.

Just two hours later, I received a reply that they liked the two chapters and their editorial team wanted to go through the entire novel. Now, that was weird. Everything looked fishy. I was unsure about sending the outcome of my tireless efforts to someone as random as a publishing house with the name of a tree.

Thanks to being in IIT, I had amazing resources in my hand. When would the top 50 in JEE contribute to society anyway? I went to Mor (that's the surname of the guy!), the biggest hacking stud of my hostel. Mor had that typical irritating nasal voice, that often sounded like the Bollywood Devdas and Paro of 50s, which often made it quite unbearable to have a conversation with him. Thank God he was in computer science, for he preferred his keyboard over his mouth.

Upon given the task, within 30 seconds, he traced the IP address of Eucalyptus and solved my confusion. 2 minutes later, he located the room where Mr. Eucalyptus was sitting. Room number ND 11, my hostel. Ishan. I patted Mor's back in appreciation and bent to touch his feet in reverence, for enlightening me with the knowledge that I needed the most that moment. I was so grateful that even his nasal 'thanks' sounded blissful.

Ishan – the same guy who once mocked my maiden attempt in front of my batchmates. It brought a strange kind of satisfaction within me, the feeling of victory over a cynic transcended through my entire soul.

I didn't bother to confront Ishan now. I just wrote back to Mr. Eucalyptus, 'I am not interested, since I have got a publisher. Now that you're so eager to read my book, I would suggest you to wait for a month or two, you can buy my book from the bookstores across the country. Thank you.'

I didn't enjoy writing my novel as much as I enjoyed writing that mail to Ishan. After fifteen minutes of my reply to him, I went to his room to check his reaction.

'Hey buddy, what's up?' I said.

'Nothing man. You say, what's up with your novel?' He said. He could not look into my eyes.

'Nothing much. It's gone for publishing.' I said, with a hidden pride.

'I got to go right now. Have to meet Rajiv.' Uncomfortable, he went out of his room on the pretext of meeting the guy next door.

19th November, 6 am IST. Yes, I was awake. As a matter of fact, I didn't sleep. I was too excited. Her first birthday. My turn to give her a surprise.

18th November, 7.30 pm US standard time. The date hadn't shifted on the other side of the globe to let me convey what I had been waiting to 'say', for so long.

I: Hey Shelley, thanks for coming online.

Shelley: Heya Kanav, it's ok. Tell me what cn I do fr u?

I: Do you have speakers in your room?

Shelley: Ya, but y?

I: Great. Could you bring Tanya to your place tomorrow?

Shelley: Oh, I see. Dnt tl me tht u r going to sing. Tanya told me tht u've a voice of a pig. :P

I: Oh, that's just in front of her. But to impress other girls, I can sing like a cuckoo. You interested?

Shelley: Wow, u r modest. However, I'm least intrstd in others' bfs.

I: Crack crack. That's my heart breaking.

Shelley: Hw cn u use cmplt wrds while typin, as if u'r a writer or smthn. Dnt u feel bored?

I: Yeah, I do feel bored, reading shorthand everywhere. :P That reminds me that in your first mail, you didn't use any shorthand. How come?

Shelley: Dey say dat 1st imprssn is d lst imprssn, I thot of ritin a frml mail. It tk me half an hr to typ dat mail. Jst kiddin!

I: *I'm completely floored by your act. First impression has been awesome.*

Shelley: *Thanx. Dnt expct me 2 flatter u nw. Anyway, wht surprise hv u planned fr hr?*

I: *Finally, you seem curious. The surprise would be unravelled only tomorrow, when she is in your room and your monitor is switched off, but the speakers and web camera are on.*

Shelley: *Intrstn! U r nt as bad as u look. :P*

I: *Yeah, I'm beautiful. Tomorrow - at what time, should I be ready with the speech of my lifetime?*

Shelley: *Aftr da classes, I'll bring hr hm. Somethin arnd 5 pm.*

I: *That's quite comfortable. That'll be 3.30 am here.*

Shelley: *U wnt hv prblm in bein 'Sleepless in hstl'. It's romantic! :P*

I: *Yeah, I don't have problems with sleeping late, only my professors do. :P*

Shelley: *LOL, u btr go n prepare ur borin' lecture! :P*

I: *Sure, make me a professor. Gn.*

Shelley: *Mornin!*

Surprised! The moment of sitting and coming up with a surprise for your beloved is perhaps the most difficult period in love life. I wanted to scribble a wonderful sonnet for her, which could tell her what she meant for me, but I was totally drained of creativity.

Not that I lacked motivation, but I clearly lacked imagination. I was facing, what could be called a lover's block. Nothing that my mind came up with came close to what I wanted. I took a deep breath, decided to close my eyes and think about what the perfect gift should be. It was already past 12 am in India and perhaps that was the reason for my lack of drive. One thing that IITians are good at is rubbing their asses and letting the shine pass on to their work at the last hour. The last hour was already over in my psychological timeframe.

I went for my classes, drowsy and came back and dropped down on the bed. I didn't do anything, put an alarm of 3 and went to sleep, thinking that the dreamworld could give me some idea for a wonderful surprise. The dream was tiresome, with the professor whom I despised most chasing me with a chainsaw, since he caught me facebooking in his class. I was petrified. The alarm, which contained one of my favorite songs that I had started hating, woke me up from the nightmare. I was relieved. It was 3 am, no more, no less.

The sudden realization that I didn't prepare anything special to mark the first birthday of my only girlfriend while she was away sent a shiver of self-hate down my spine. I switched on my computer, hoping to pen down another poem for the rhythm of my life.

I opened the word processor, began doodling...

~~Things change, people derange~~

~~One remains same, lame lame lame!~~

Suddenly, I received an incoming chat on skype. It was Shelley.

My thrill was back while I chucked my lame poem away in the recycle bin.

Shelley: Hey, ur Tanya is gonna b hr ne moment nw. She hrslf wntd 2 chat wid u, dat's y she's comin. wht shud I do?

I: Switch on the web camera and connect the speakers. My lecture will begin as soon as she comes! Position the camera in such a way that it gives me a full room view.

Shelley: Dnt u thnk dat I myt hv prblm wid letting a guy c my bedroom.

I: Hide your stuff. I am not peeping through your window.

Shelley: Ya, I use a mac. :P Oh she's here. I'm connectin u.

I: Switch the monitor off.

The network was established. I could see through the globe to the other side. It was a not-so-messy room, with posters of Robert Pattinson all across the walls and some shabby clothes on her bed, which were a bit 'oh-that's-how-it-looks' for an inexperienced unexposed novice like me. There was a commotion outside the room, with occasional accented girly screams like 'Happy birthday' or 'Yo, wow, you are 18, amazing!' or compliments like 'You look stunning!' etc. making my desperation to see her face climb the charts.

The moment that my eyes were crazily waiting for, for the last three months seemed to be seconds away. I was lustful. I could feel it. She was already there in my imagination. I was just waiting for her to be there in front of my eyes.

The 'hulchul' outside the room barbarously played with my

eagerness. I was inwardly cursing Shelley for taking so much time to let my beloved come to meet me. The wait ended when I saw those soft feet wrapped in the red threads of beautiful stilettos entering through the main door. My eyes almost popped out and tried to enter my laptop screen. It was of no use. The careful walk with those newly bought stilettos, the blue one-piece ending millimeters above her knee, the ribbon tied tightly across her waist, the straps lucky enough to be proudly hanging on the prettiest shoulders ever, and the gleaming face with a scintilating smile, but worried eyes, seemingly devoid of joy captivated me. Or was the last bit a figment of my imagination? She looked the same, while I felt like I had aged in the last three months. Her eyes had developed dark circles round them, giving me a hint of her sleepless nights. She had put a little bit of make-up, something that she had always detested, to hide the circles encapsulating the pain of her love life.

She came and sat directly across the PC, her back facing the camera. Her hair was tied up in a single knot, which allowed me to look at her neck. It was the first time I was observing her neck, the place where she was most ticklish. I wanted to poke her. I wanted to surprise her.

I exclaimed to myself, 'Alas, the technology hasn't advanced so much to make apparition possible. Until IITians pay more heed to technology than girls, apparition would remain an unattainable dream.' The last thought made me chuckle. I went back to the work that kept my sweaty face hooked to a screen – the screen that beheld the sight of my beloved.

'Hey, you know what? Jainesh, the hunk kinda' guy who lives next door, came up to me and wished me. His intentions seemed dicey; I didn't give him any importance but engaged him in a conversation. Meanwhile, Paritosh came and literally raped him!' Her voice was excited. She seemed cheerful. The sadness in her eyes was actually a figment of my imagination. She was happy. And I felt cheated with every sound of the enchanting laughter that struck my ears.

'Beauty lies in the eyes of the lecher.' Shelley commented and both of them giggled. Two girls laughing is a pleasant sight, provided you know that they're not laughing at you. My self-doubt erupted.

'Hey, let me get to the main reason why I am here! Did Kanav mail anything to me, Shelley, did you check my inbox?' Tanya asked. She was expecting something.

'Yeah, I did, around 15 minutes ago. There was no mail from his side.' Shelley answered.

'What the hell! These guys can never walk an extra mile for their girl.' Tanya said, frustrated. I felt delighted, it was time to clear my throat and impress the chick with my extempore.

'I did so much for him. He didn't even bother to write a simple mail.' Tanya said in disgust. 'Let me check the mail once again, what if God has been kind to me.'

She turned towards me. She looked stunning. Jesus! She was advancing towards the PC; she was going to spoil my surprise.

'TANYA!' Shelley exclaimed and rushed to hold Tanya from the back by her dress, while Tanya moved ahead letting the straps that once hung on her shoulders now get snarled in her hip bone, and she, with her entire 'weight', fell just in front of the web-camera. I was bewildered at the sudden outcome of the events. There she was, topless and mortified, without a hint that her lover on the other side of the planet had turned into a statue. Little did I know that I would get a return gift even before I could give her a birthday gift.

She immediately got up, embarrassingly pulled her apparel up and positioned herself back to normal. Meanwhile, Shelley started chanting the 'Eeks...sorry' mantra. I thanked God for creating such a thing as wardrobe malfunction. It's a boon in disguise, for boyfriends whose girlfriends are stern and unattainable. Tanya shyly said, 'It's okay.'

Just at the moment, I switched on my microphone and began my extempore. 'After two months, I saw my Bubu today, literally. I never knew why I loved you, but now I know.'

There was no response from their side. They started talking.

'Why did you stop me?' Tanya questioned.

'Oh, just to ...' Shelley stammered, 'no, don't take it that way. It was not my intention, just wanted to...yes I remember now, I wanted to switch on the AC before you sit at the PC, you know. Computers radiate heat, you know, don't you?'

'You're acting creepy.' Tanya said, with a suspicious look in her eyes.

'Oh no, I'm embarrassed at what happened and I feel bad that it happened.' Shelley said with a shy smile. She moved towards me.

'Ah, I switched on the AC and also the speakers, which were switched off till now, if you understand what I mean,' she spoke the last line looking at the camera.

WTF! The whole idea of sparking off an intimate boob-filled conversation went in vain. I had to start again, and be spontaneous. I decided to try out something completely different. I sang. Ok, I won't boast. I just played the most suited song for the occasion in my speakers and placed my microphone in front of it. Bryan Adams singing -

'I want to be your hot-tub, when you dip in
I want to be your bathrobe, when you drip in,
I want to be your coffee, when you sip in
I want to be - your underwear!'

The faces that were trying to get back to normal mood became scandalized once again. It was like Shelley had planned this song to woo Tanya. Tanya was dumbfounded and she looked at the speakers, when Shelley waved her hands at the camera with a 'What the hell are you doing?' expression on her troubled face.

'Shelley, what is this? You're scaring me.' Tanya exclaimed.

'It's not me, it's ...' Shelley was interrupted.

'It's not Shelley my dear lady, it's your Bubu reporting live from Delhi.' I said in Navjot Singh Sidhu's voice, and continued, 'It's 4.30 in the morning, Delhi seems very lonely, with all the hot chicks and real 'booboos' transported to America. Recently, there has been a case of cyber-flashing in Northampton, where a very ravishing girl flashed her 'teeth' to her horny boyfriend in Delhi over internet. The boy has become so happy that he ran topless across his hostel corridor two times singing, "Happy birthday to you, happy birthday to you."'

'Jesus! What's this? Kanav, where is he? Is he in the room?' Tanya hollered.

'Yes, find me.' I said.

She jumped from the chair and started running across the room. She searched for me in the cupboards, below the tables, beneath the bed. I relished the sight, especially the last two. She was hyperactive. What fun is it to have a naive girlfriend!

I started laughing. Uncontrollably. She got more and more frustrated, with a wishful frenzy highlighting her pretty face, until she realized that the virtual world contained her real world. She came right near the monitor, right at the moment when I began...

Find me here, find me there
The world is too big to scan
When you find me, you would hear
That, it was all part of a plan! Happy Birthday.

She switched on the monitor and her worried face, which was excited a moment before, burst into tears seeing my face. She started sobbing. She was right across me; staring at me with a look that makes me cry everytime I remember it. Even now. Her tears flowed like rain from a dark cloud. All her foundation cream was washed away in the saline outburst, making a muddy strain of fluid running down her neck and throat. I was enraptured, staring without a blink, until my eyes welled up and became inundated due to air-friction. I realized that she wouldn't stop if I didn't make her stop.

'Come on, your make-up is being washed away. I wouldn't talk to you if you look so ugly.' I remarked.

She grinned. She was crying nevertheless. She was laughing and crying at the same time. It was weird. It was so not lovable. It was insane. Girls might have termed it as 'cute'.

'Look who's talking. The blank screen was better than your face.' She taunted, crying. It was the first time that we had talked face to face after our last date. It was the second time there was a smile on my face that was complete. It was the third time that I felt that hope never goes in vain. And it was the millionth time I felt proud to be in love.

Meanwhile, I saw Shelley leaving her room, giving us privacy. Tanya's tears had subsided, she lifted her skirt up to wipe it from the face. 'Enjoy the view,' she said with a mischievous smile.

'I love white.' I said, dazzled.

'You better do.'

'You seem *meherbaan* today. What's the reason?'

'Nothing. I've become a slut, in US.' She said, casually. She was back to normal, with not-so-dark circles encircling the two most precious jewels in this world.

'That's not funny. How would you feel if I say the same?' I retorted.

'What - that you're a slut? Oh come on, I know that no-one will give you any *bhav.*'

'You know me very well, don't you?'

'No, I know other girls pretty well.' She said with a wink.

'How are you?' I said, with the sentimental mood setting in.

'I'm okay. I can't tell you how badly I missed you all this while. Every time I think about our first day together, I start crying. It has been months since I slept properly.'

'I'm so sorry for making you go through all this.' I said.

'Don't start seeking sympathy, you dumbass! I've limited time; let's make the maximum of it.'

'Let's make out.' I said, with a devilish smile.

'I've already exposed everything I had. So...'

'So, should I commence the sacred task?'

'No, now that I have seen your face, I think I've completed my quota of seeing ugly things for the day.'

'Hmm. So what should we talk about?'

'How silly you are! Talk about you, talk about me and talk about us. And if you can't just keep quiet and listen to me.' Tanya said.

I chose the latter option. It was the easiest one. She chatted. She talked about her life, her relatives, her mother, her college and her friends. I was happy to see her happy. She had almost got acclimatized to the new environment. In short, she made it obvious that I was useless. Okay, I'm overreacting, but that's what I felt that time. I felt stifled. Perhaps, I didn't want to see her happy. I wanted her to be in agony, because of my absence in her life. I wanted to feel important, just like she was important to me.

'Are you happy?' I asked finally, breaking her chirpy monologue.

'Now that I've seen you, yes I am.'

'No don't beat about the bush.' I chided.

'Everybody is beating Bush. We're hoping for a new President soon.'

'Stop acting smart! I'm tired of your meaningless humour. If you can't talk straight, don't talk to me.' I yelled irritably.

'Okay.' She said and disconnected the video chat.

I was frustrated. It was our first fight. And, it was abrupt. It was 5 am and my back was breaking from the last one and half hour of idling. I looked outside. It was still dark. I desperately wanted to talk to her. But my ego didn't allow me. I went outside to catch some fresh air, but the early morning lull seemed too torturous for me to step out of my room. I came back and sat down, my mind swinging like a pendulum whether to connect or not to connect. I took my pen and paper and started scribbling my feelings for her. They say writing is man's most faithful confidant. It turned out to be one of the best poems written by me and it softened my mood miraculously. Now I wanted to recite that to her.

I set my ego aside and reconnected. The screen quivered a little and I could see Shelley in front of me.

'What happened? Where's Tanya?' I asked, nettled.

'She says that you'd asked her to not talk to you. So, she's not talking.' Shelley replied.

My irritation catapulted. But, I had no other option other than talking to her. She was the cause as well as cure of my annoyance.

'Tell her that she wasn't giving straight answers to my questions, that's why I got pissed.'

'Had you been straight, I would have given you straight answers.' I heard a voice from somewhere.

'Tanya, this is not right. Do you know what my condition has been throughout? I've spent each and every moment thinking about you, feeling so empty from within that I had to ...' I had the urge to tell her about the book, but it was not the right time.

'That I had to...?' She questioned.

'That I had to sleep with other women to get over you.' I said to avoid the surprise. But the pause and the force in my voice gave her a stunner.

'What did you say?'

'I said that I had to sleep with other women to get over you.' I repeated, with as serious a look as I could have made out of my 'funny' face.

'Oh really. Who were they? Blind girls?'

'No, just dumb bimbos like you.' I winked.

'WTH! Can't you talk straight?' Tanya said, irritably and then burst out laughing at the realization of the existence of a vicious circle.

'What goes around comes back around. In thy face.'

'Okay, tell me what you were asking.'

'I just want to know how much you miss me. Do you even miss

me? Am I of any value to you? And if yes, what are your plans to keep me happy? I can't wait for months to have a chat with you.'

'Wait wait wait. You're going too fast. Wait a minute let me answer one by one. So, I miss you a lot. In classes, my notebooks contain you; at home my mind; in sleep, my dreams and in sleeplessness, my imagination. See, I've become poetic.'

'Pleased. So what are your plans to keep me happy?'

'I'm going to keep you happy by keeping myself happy. That's all I can do for you right now and that's all I expect you to do for me. In this situation, we need to be strong and determined to keep each other happy by keeping ourselves happy. See, have I not gotten smart lately? It's all due to respite from your company.'

I reciprocated with an empty self-pacifying grin. She was right. She was mature. She was actually smart, while I was being childish.

'*Acchha*, in all these emotional talk, you made me forget about my birthday gift. Where's my birthday gift?' She broke my concentration.

'Oh, you remember it. Do you really want to see it? I thought now that you've forgotten, I would have recycled it in future.'

'No, I've a very sharp memory when it comes to birthday gifts.'

'Great. So let me stand.' I said, in a naughty tone.

'Oh my god, what are you up to? I don't want that.' She screamed.

'Ok, I won't recite the poem that I'd written for you. Dirty mind!'

'Poem?'

'Yes, I wrote a poem for you.'

'Oh really? You're making my day.'

'Now that you have raided my night.'

'Wow, that's romantic.' She gave me the most endearing smile ever.

'Here goes the romantic *cheezon-ka-baap*!'

This composition is called 'A Simple Wish'. It's dedicated to the love of my life, Tanya Mehra, who is eagerly waiting to hear what my simple wish sounds like. (She was smiling!)

I've a simple wish
To begin each morning
Seeing your smile

I've a simple wish
To breathe your fragrance
From a thousand miles
(provided you take bath daily!)

I can see your eyes
With my eyes closed.
I can feel your breath
When the wind lows.
I can hear your voice
In my every dream.
I can see your face
Far but still full of gleam.

I've a simple wish
To make you my muse
With every passing moment

I've a simple wish
To make you laugh a thousand times
For each of the tears that went

You're the reason
For me and for everything.
You're in all the seasons
Be it winter or spring.

You're the words
That come out of my mind.
You are that little bird
Who is one of a kind

I've a simple wish
To touch the sky and the moon
With you by my side.

I've a simple wish
To live that fulfilling life soon
Which only you could provide.

Just look at me once.

And feel my love for you.
For, I've just a simple wish -
To make you joyous - with me too!

I looked up from the paper with an I-know-I-rocked-it feeling at the computer screen. She was crying. She was crying out loudly. I was dumbstruck. I had such a crybaby for a girlfriend.

'What happened?' I interrogated.

'Nothing. You're the most wonderful person on this planet.' She said wiping her nose. Her nose has become red and her cheeks had turned pink. She was looking so adorable that if she had been near me I would have wrapped my arms around her, only if she could assure me that her dripping nose wouldn't be wiped on my shirt.

'Why don't you wipe your nose once again, like you did before?' I flirted.

'You like white, don't you?' She asked sensuously.

'Sure, I do.' I said, eagerly.

She took out a white handkerchief from her pocket and wiped her nose, flushing my innate desire down the drain.

'You surely love white.' She winked and continued, 'by the way, I didn't hear from you about the return gift that you'd already received.'

'What return gift?'

'Didn't it knock your head till now?' She twitched her bosom a little.

'Oh, those! They were pretty...' I stumbled to collect my words, 'delicious.'

'We're done for the day, Mr. Bajaj. Thank you for your time.' Tanya said and waved a bye.

'Hey, wait a minute. Can you get me those return gifts, once again? Please.' I pleaded, with my eyeballs pulled down by gravity.

'No. Good things should come in small quantity. They're valued that way. I do have another surprise for you. I'm coming back to India in Feb, in my semester break.' She said.

'Wow, delicious!' I said.

She pulled her one piece down from the left side and whispered, 'The next one, the next time,' and resigned from Skype.

My happiness knew no bounds. Why? You know why! I realized the value of happy endings. If all the movies of Bollywood ended with a boob flash, I could just imagine how happy the perverted crowd would have been. People, like me - trust me more than half of India is like me, would have fast forwarded such movies on their laptops just to watch those last 30 seconds of glory.

I kissed my laptop screen that beheld the first sight of those heavenly bodies and walked in a state of wishful thinking, a euphemism for fantasy. It was a deep and 'fluffy' sleep. You might be thinking that I'm a pervert. But believe me, every guy is the same, no matter how much mahatma he poses to be. If locked in a room filled with porn *dvds* and Robin Sharma's books, I bet that any man 'man enough' would first go for the prior. No monk wants to sell his Ferrari, without making out on its backseat.

There was one more return gift awaiting my inbox. When I got up from the fluffy pillows cradling my fluffy dreams full of fluffy things, I went to brush my teeth. In the washroom, there was a buzz. Someone told me that Anuj had got a fully paid internship offer at MIT and was so delighted last night that he drank thirteen pegs of Vodka. He was vomiting for the last one hour. I felt jealous. It was I whose girlfriend lived in US and this desperado gets an opportunity to spend two bloody months in US, that too without any *kharcha*. Lucky bastard! Let him puke and die!

'Dude, keep shitting through your mouth! Prove to us that you're an asshole.' I shouted and returned to my room.

I thought about what I intended to do, why the hell did I not apply for internships till date, despite that early advice by Sameer. I felt envious.

Irritated, I went back to my room. Unclear about what to do, I decided to pay my homage to my goddess. My attention shifted from Anuj to my digital temple, where I had earlier come face to face what they would call godliness. So intensely was I mesmerized with the majesty of those natural gifts that even the boot-screen seemed like a boob-screen to me.

I felt cheerful. I looked out through the window, trying to pass a smile to my best friend for-never, however the sky seemed empty - and boring, like most of the Gods are. Irked by sky, I resumed the session on Skype. There was stark emptiness there too. Things turned out to be boring on that Thursday. I had a class in half an hour and I was squandering time over the internet.

Before going, I decided to check my mail once, where it turned out that there was something bigger than her majesty awaiting for me. It was a letter. It was a long awaited mail from one of the publishers whom I wrote to around a month before.

Dear Kanav,

Thanks for writing to us. Our editorial team went through your work and they liked your style, the intensity of humour and the passion reflected in your writing. They however concluded that the content has childishness associated with it, which actually worked for you since it added an innate humour to your work. We are delighted to consider your work for publishing. Congratulations!

Please meet us at our office in Karol Bagh as soon as you can to proceed with the formalities.

Regards,
Anirudh Singh
Editor
Karma Publishers

I was euphoric. Karma was a good name in the publishing world, especially known for encouraging young writers. I immediately picked up my phone and unconsciously dialled Tanya's Indian number, which rang, until I realized what I had done. Her phone was alive.

A moment later, I received a call back. I didn't realize when and how did my euphoria turn into frenzy. It was the person who played the villain in my first book, on the other side of the phone.

'Hello, I received a call from this number. Who do you want to talk to?' The intimidating voice said in the most nefarious tone ever.

'Aaa...' I mumbled and changed my accent to much like Lalu Prasad Yadav and said, *'Hum Bihar se Jamuna babu bol rahe hain. Ramji se baat ho sakat hai kaa?'*

I heard a riotous laughter from the other side. She replies, *'Ramji Sita ko lane Lanka gaye hain. Hanuman ko call kar lo.'*

I was stunned. After thinking over whatever happened, I rolled on the floor and laughed uncontrollably. My friends assembled in the room to watch my early morning show, which they thought was hysteria. I was so badly tickled that my laugh took over a minute to let my breath catch up.

Having a stern to be mother-in-law bestowed with a sense of humour is the least you would expect in this world, especially after getting boxed by her hand on your left cheek, oh wait, the right cheek I guess. I don't remember. I believe in forgive and forget, you see. I couldn't believe it was the same person who I had encountered once. From her voice, I was dead sure that it was her. I just couldn't wait to share it with Tanya.

It was a funny start to the day. I got over the jealousy over Anuj, received a publishing contract, had fun with my to-be mother-in-law, hopefully and rolled over the dirtiest floor on this planet, bruising my back. Excitedly, I went to the classroom and attended my lecture with rapt attention, surrounded by occasional streaks of laughter.

My professor caught me smiling bizarrely and asked me the reason of my happiness. I smiled more, the whole class reciprocated. He asked again, I showed all my teeth. He realized that either he was deaf or I was dumb, despite being well endowed with teeth and the wire-frame, and decided to concentrate on more significant topics than my villainous mother-in-law.

The class ended, I rushed to meet Mr. Singh, with Aryan, once again. It was a lively meeting. The agreement was encouraging and genuine. Aryan's favorite finger didn't need to dance to his tunes. Mr. Singh touched my heart, when he said, 'Don't just sign the agreement; give an autograph. You're going to be giving your autographs on a lot of copies very soon.'

I felt proud. I had a talent and it was going to be recognized by people around. The title of the book was still a thing to worry about since my publisher didn't approve of 'Kismat Disconnection' and my friends were 'trying to' help me with it.

'What's wrong with the title?' Anuj asked, in an American accent intentionally, to flaunt his recent achievement.

'The movie didn't do well at the box office. I'm just feeling superstitious.' I said, quite genuinely.

'Wait, I'll find a good title for your book. How about – "Fuck! I couldn't fuck"?' Anuj said, to everyone's delight. There is something with the F word, it lights up dull faces. The word seems to have the power to satisfy voyeuristic tendencies in the souls around.

'What the fuck!' I said, disgusted.

'It's an awesome title.' Aryan said.

'Go write a book yourself with that title. I prefer using 'oops' instead of the F word.' I said.

'You've it. Oops! She kicked my balls and ran away...' Anuj said and realized that he hit a wrong chord. He immediately apologized.

'Oops sounds cool. Oops it is. "Oops! I fell in love!".' I said.

'Catchy enough.' Aryan gave the green signal.

Sameer, who had not been around, entered my room just then. He exclaimed, 'Wow, the trio is here. It has been days since we all hung out together.'

'Now don't start showcasing your homosexual sentiments.' Anuj remarked. Aryan cracked a mouthfart while I, passed an inward smile. Sameer, with his sorry face, tried to seek some sympathy, but in vain.

'So Sameer, how is Reva?'

'Oh, you know what? She just had a break-up. You know the reason of her break-up?'

And thus, Sameer commenced yet another tale about him and his queen. And we listened, enthralled, for the very first time. The story had all it takes to make a perfect Bollywood flick.

'Reva called me last night and asked me to come to the institute, to study together. I was perplexed, that suddenly, after such a long time how she could remember me. I went to the institute. She was waiting for me near the wind-tunnel, in her track suit.'

'Did you plan to do PT together, thereafter?' Anuj joked, to nobody's joy.

'Yes, how could you guess that, asshole!' Sameer remarked.

'So I reached the wind-t. As I observed her face carefully, I realized that she looked devastated. I asked her what had happened to her. She didn't say a word. She grabbed my sleeve with her right hand and dragged me ahead. I kept on asking her what had happened. She didn't say a word.'

'First tell me, did you guys make out? Only then would I listen.' Anuj said. Everyone was so engrossed in Sameer's tale that nobody paid heed to the pervert.

'She took me to Block one and climbed up the stairs to its top floor. It was totally abandoned, having a distinctly haunted feel.'

'After all it was 'surrounded' by Reva walking, like a ghost, in her loose track-suit.' Aryan said with a wink.

'She is not as fat as you think.' Sameer said plainly.

'God, it seems that you know her very closely.' Anuj said and gave a high-five to Aryan. I was more interested in what happened next, since the story-teller in me was eager to add a story in the sequel to my first book, therefore I hurried Sameer to continue with his story.

'We went to a deserted room where she started crying. I didn't know what was happening. I got very nervous, my heart was pounding. I hesitantly wiped her tears with my right hand, when she jumped and hugged me. She was still sobbing. I was puzzled. And to add to the misery, I got aroused. I twisted by body from my waist, in a helix like a DNA.'

'The fattest DNA ever.'Anuj continued with his mockery.

'Thank you. I was glad when I got free from her arms. I asked her why she was unhappy. She didn't say anything for a while and then suddenly, she said that she had cheated on her boyfriend Siddharth.'

'Oh...f…!' I exlaimed, unconsciously.

'That's what! She cheated. But with whom? I didn't dare to ask.' Sameer said.

'Gosh, she doesn't look like such a big stud.' Aryan said.

'Yes, she doesn't. She stopped crying and came really close to me. I felt awkward.' Sameer said.

'Awkward or aroused?'Anuj asked.

'Both. And then she asks me whether I considered her a slut. I was speechless.'

'Did you tell her that you did consider her one?' Anuj asked, curiously.

'I didn't. But now I do. She came very close to me and asked whether I liked her. I couldn't say a word. She touched my cheek and a moment later, we kissed.'

'*Ye baat! Jeeo mere laal.* Finally, you prove that you're not gay, you're a lesbian!' Anuj shrieked, provoking a riotous laughter amongst us.

'Funny, ha! She asked me next whether I liked her or not. I nodded. Thanks to the proximity, I could dare to ask her who she cheated Siddharth with. She replied that he was someone whom I know very well. And lo, there was the apprehension that – bloody hell, she made out with my friend! The dread disgusted me and I returned to the hostel, without moving ahead with her any further. I haven't talked to her thereafter. Who amongst you dogs is the one? Tell me.'

'Had it been any hot chick, I would have been the first one to take responsibility even if it hadn't been me. But for Reva, eeks.'

'Wait a minute. It's you who's the lucky bastard!' I exclaimed at Sameer, when the dawn of deduction struck my mind.

'Bloody shit!' Aryan and Sameer exclaimed at the same time.

It was the realization that shocked each and every cell of our bodies. Sameer was almost close to fainting, his mouth gaping and eyes dilated, looking like a statue of a sumo wrestler. Anuj, silent like the characters in movies of 1800s, could not throw any sarcastic taunts for the occasion. Aryan, though stunned, had a weird smile on his face, whereas I was amazed at the climax of the story. My respect for Reva became tenfold; she could be the most befitting character in my future writing pursuits.

'By the way, now you can talk and do much more with her. Leave us to get disgusted with you and her.' Aryan commented wickedly.

Sameer walked back to his room, his chatterbox tongue forgot how to engineer words. He felt bizarre, like all of us. I was happy. I got a story to tell, a catchy title for my book and the amazement of my book getting published in my head.

Second year of our college is the idlest period of our college life. Friendship gets fragmented, due to departmental courses and personal discourses, interest in academics is at nadir, since the majority of the professors in the first year seemed to have sucked every drop of interest that remains in studying, and moreover there are no adjustment issues or job pressures. Majority of IITians discover these three amazing ways to pass their time in IIT:

a. Sleeping in lectures with occasional absence

b. Watching sitcoms with occasional porn on their hostel LAN

c. Leching at hot chicks in real as well as virtual world with occasional hook-ups and hiccups

I don't know about other colleges, but I guess the case would be the same everywhere. I was in a somewhat similar circumstance in November 2008, with my love life looking pale and hope of getting back together, vanishing at the speed of light. Even porn didn't excite me anymore, after seeing some real things in life. Leching was a considerable option, but nobody seemed appealing, no matter how well my friends rated them, when compared to Tanya. Beauty lies in the eyes of the lecher, as Shelley said.

Lectures started to seem interesting as I developed interest in a course on Entrepreneurial Management. For the first time in college, I found a professor who knew what students wanted. Sex. His name was Professor Verghese, popularly known as Virgo amongst students. He found analogies of every topic with the grand topic of life creation.

One of his classic depiction on starting-up goes like this:

'Starting up is like your first time. You're unsure of your partner and your own ability. You doubt whether you'll be able to deliver your best in the first go. You have to trust your gut instinct and only if both of you are prepared, you should shoot at the aim. Many entrepreneurs fail just because they haven't taken ample safety precautions before plunging straightaway. It's a creative job; you require passion, tenderness as well as vigour to make the best of the experience. And mistakes do happen, don't worry if they do, they're exciting. It's fun coining their names beforehand.'

Owing to my unwavering interest in sexology, I attended all the lectures and managed to secure the maximum grade possible.

December 6th

After the examination got over, my professor called four students from our class to his room. He offered us an opportunity to attend University of Massachusets's Entrepreneurial Summit, with a clause that only one amongst us was to be selected. He planned to take a written interview.

On the day of the interview, Virgo asked us just one question:

Why should we not select you for the Summit?

I couldn't think of an answer. Not that I'm perfect, but because I was so imperfect, that I couldn't find the biggest negative point in me. I decided to choose the easiest path – the path of honesty.

My reply followed:

I should not be selected because the main reason for my applying is not my interest in entrepreneurship but that I want to meet my girlfriend, who lives in Northampton, in Massachusets.

I didn't know whether I did the right thing or not, but I felt really light from within. I discussed with other classmates of mine regarding the answers that they wrote. Their replies were really scary. One of them wrote that he should not be selected because he would give other participants an inferiority complex. An hour later, after each one of us submitted the answers, Virgo called me into his room. I was the first one to be called.

'So what's her name?' Virgo asked.

'Tanya.' I answered.

'Where did you find her? Internet?'

'No, at a friend's birthday party.'

'Indian?'

'Yes, sir. From Delhi.'

'Who's the villain then? Why's she in US?'

'Her mom caught us.'

'Doing what?'

'Umm...Nothing...' I said shyly.

'What did she catch then? Come on, tell me.'

'Sir, we were kissing.' I mumbled, looking at my feet. My ears had turned red. It was one of the most embarrassing moments of my life – confiding my romantic endeavours to a person of my father's age.

'I'm proud of you.' Virgo said.

Virgo came out of his chamber and greeted the other guys, 'Unfortunately, entrepreneurship requires passion and passion requires love. Unfortunately, your answers perfectly convinced me about why I should not choose you. Kanav's going to US. Thanks guys for your interest.'

My ass caught fire. Not literally, though. I was running as if my ass had caught fire. I ran across the main floors of the multi storied building, at one point just managing not to collide with my professor, and entered the computer services centre. I wanted to convey this to my beloved as soon as possible that eight months from now, I would be spending two weeks with her. The thought itself gave me goosebumps.

As soon as I reached the PC, a strange hiccup halted my enthusiasm. The funny noise brought the mischief within me and I decided that I would surprise her, rather than telling her beforehand. She was anyway coming to India in Feb, so my desire to meet her would already be fulfilled.

I called my mother to give her the good news. I had never heard her sounding so happy.

'Hi Ma, I just got selected for an entrepreneurial summit in Massachusets. I've to go to US in Aug, for two weeks. I'm the only guy who got selected.'

'Wow beta, you made our entire 'khandaan' proud. You know what? You're the first person to go to a foreign country in our family.'

'I know Ma. It's a proud moment for me as well.'

'I'll give you the best food for those two weeks, full of *gujiyas*, *mathris* and *achar. Acha*, don't forget to carry chawanprash and some *badams*, it'll keep your mind active all throughout.'

I was to go to US eight months from now, but my mother had already started packing my bags in her mind.

'Ma, we'll decide it then, why are you bothering yourself now? It's almost 8 months away.'

'Oh, what if I forget, I'll make a list right now and mention all these things there. I'll keep on adding things as and when they strike my mind. I don't want you to be hungry in that *firang* land.'

'Oh Ma, they've a weight limit to the amount of luggage that we carry.'

'How could they do that? *Arey bhai*, when you're going to an entirely new country for two weeks, how could they stop you from taking the necessary food. I'll talk to the airport officials.'

'Ma, they have fixed rules.' I said.

'How could they be so ruthless? I'll lodge a complaint right now to allow students to take more luggage than others, it'll get changed by August.'

'Ma, *chill maaro*.' I said, thrilled by her anxiety.

'What is this *chill maaro* that you keep saying all the time? *Dilli ne bhasha bigad di hai tumhari!*' She reprimanded.

'Oh ma, I'm going. Tell Dad the good news. Bye, take care.' I said.

It was one surprise that I shared with her which made my Mom so worried and anxious. The mere thought of what would happen when I would tell them that I've written a love story which was going to be published made my feet run cold. My parents are progressive and can be termed in *Dilli-ki-bhasha* as 'cool', but they consider me like a prodigious 5 year old kid, who needs special care and concern all the time and needs to be spoonfed every little thing that he requires and utterly despises, like *chawanprash* and *amle-ka-murabba*.

A quiver tickled me at a very wrong place. It was my cell in my pocket and it was Ma on the other side. Curious, I picked up the phone.

'Hi Ma!'

'*Beta*, I just read the luggage limits on google and even consulted your Dad. Your Dad and I have an amazing idea. I am going to accompany you to the US. That way we could carry twice the luggage and you would not have to worry about food. At the same time, I would get a chance to visit America.'

Jesus! I could not believe what I had heard. The canvas on which I had painted my hopes seemed to have caught fire. Speechless, I relied on an expression called 'hmm' – which happens to be my favourite word during hard times.

'Hmm Ma, we'll see.' I said, hoping that time would lower her enthusiasm of a *videsh-yatra*.

'Your Dad has already hired an agent for passport.' My mother said. She was giving me shock after shock. I could not believe that God had started wrestling with me once again, this time hiring my mother as the adversary.

'Great. We'll talk later, my tongue is itching, I need to scratch it.' I disconnected the phone in irritation, making a weird excuse.

Time ran by like a jet swooshing across the sky, leaving behind a tail of a weird shape. My exams were over and my girlfriend got busy after her birthday, as her maternal enemy Paritosh had increased the restrictions on her, after my accidental call to her hilarious mother, who sent Ramji to Lanka. I was surprised that she remembered my number and still cracked that joke, perhaps just to make fun of me. I like humour, but I don't like it when it is directed at me and that too by a person who is an epitome of villainy for me.

I went home during the winter vacations. Since there was no Tanya around to spend my left-over bucks on my home shopping assignments, I ended up displeasing my mother. I preferred sitting and idling around at home than shopping for daily groceries, which disappointed my mother. She complained that I had become lazier than my previous summer self. My mom's enthusiasm of accompanying me to US didn't waver a bit and she was half way through the passport processing.

I carefully avoided the mention of my novel at home, since it would make them curious to read it and I feared that they would ask me change the plot significantly. I thought of surprising them when it got published.

Mr. Singh, from Karma publishers, had promised that the novel, after typesetting and editing would get into print by February, which left me ample time to prepare my launch as an author and anticipate the fame and little astonishment, amongst my peers. I made the cover page myself, and tried to make it look as weird as possible. I considered my book to be a weird love story, so the cover needed to suit its image. While I was giving the final touch to the cover of my book, my father accidentally caught me designing it. The colours attracted him to my computer screen and the title with my name at the bottom provoked him to interrogate me thoroughly.

'What's this? Have you written a book?' My Dad asked, puzzled at the discovery.

I felt really shy. It seemed like he had caught me at the most 'intricate' position in my previous book. I didn't say a word, looked down at my feet, which had long crooked nails, and smiled placidly. My mind went to a dozen guilt trips at the instant I was questioned. My Dad has this deep baritone, exactly like *Jagjit Singh*, which when serious can make you feel scared, despite the fact that he is perhaps the coolest Dad on this planet.

'What happened? You didn't bother to tell me.' He interrogated, with the hint of a smile. I heaved a deep sigh.

'However, the title sounds exciting!' My Dad exclaimed and in a very serene voice, 'Is it autobiographical?'

'No, it's fictitious. Last semester, I just heard too many stories, so I decided to pen it down.' I lied hesitantly. But my Dad, being an avid storyteller himself, could easily spot the incongruency in my body language.

'First books are always autobiographical. Even if you don't want to write about yourself, you unconsciously fulfill all your wishes through the protagonist.' He said.

This was getting weird. If he read my book, the kind of wishes that I fulfilled through my protagonist would have spoilt the ideal-son image that he had about me in his mind. I didn't say a word.

'Come on, give me the manuscript. Let me read how my son fell in love.' He asked. I felt choked. I wanted to rush to the toilet and drown myself inside the commode.

The passion that I had discovered for writing seemed to have become the most embarrassing discovery in my life. How could I face my father when he read the intimate scene that his son had written? It was as embarrassing as being caught watching Fashion TV's midnight hot programme, muted, stealthily at night, a real life experience which I wouldn't like to recount here.

'Dad, no. It's not for you. It's for youngsters. You wouldn't like it.' I said. Dad was stunned.

'Why? You think I'm old!' He teased.

'No, I didn't mean it that way. I just meant that ... it's amateurish and childish ... it's made for college-students.' I uttered, helplessly.

'Do you like it?' He asked.

'Yes.' I answered, consciously. I looked at the design of the cover on the screen. I had a wide smile on my face. One's child, no matter how it looks, always brings a smile on your face when one sees it. I looked back at my father. Even he was smiling.

'Great. It ought to be great then. Let me go through the manuscript.' He said.

'No. You read it once it gets published.' I said, with force.

'Wow, you found a publisher as well. I'm proud of you, son. I'll read it when you feel it's the right time.' He said, suppressing his eagerness.

'I am very anxious about how it will be received.' I said.

'Make them laugh. They'll like you.' My Dad said.

That was the best advice that any writer could get. I smiled at my father, who patted me lightly on the head.

'Dad, promise me that you won't tell Mom about it until it gets published.' I pleaded, since I feared that my mother would start publicising amongst her friends, whom I didn't want to get scandalized reading my book.

'Oh don't worry, she is already busy publicising her US trip with you.' He said, with a cute grin. I felt like fainting in vexation.

The winter vacations were spent in a thrilling atmosphere. My sister became the first one from my family to read my book. She was so shocked to discover what her so-called 'ideal brother' had written that she couldn't say anything more than 'Oh my God', in response to my novel. Later, she told me that she liked it but couldn't believe that I could write it, since the adventures seemed so-not-me.

On the way back, I contemplated about the last one month that I had spent at home. I realized that I had learnt four things during that time:

- It's blissful to have cool parents, who're eagerly waiting to accompany you to your date on the other side of the earth

- It's very difficult to manage two girls at the same time, especially when both of them are your younger sisters. My four years old cousin sister visited us during the vacation

- If you want to make someone hate you, force them to eat *chawanprash* twice a day, provided you're not that someone's mother

- Hostel-life overtakes home in just one aspect, you don't have to bathe daily in chilly winter

Just when I reached my hostel, I faced a severe shock. My most precious asset was stolen. The New Year didn't look promising. The ice-cream cone that I'd saved as a souvenir from my first date had been broken into pieces. Thanks to the ants. They had eaten up every little bit of my memories that were contained in that little piece of wafer. And, they were still not happy. They were circumscribing it, trying to take every little atom of my love attached to it. Perturbed, I put a glass of water on it and mercilessly saw those little creatures floating, fighting hard to liberate themselves of the sudden calamity. They couldn't. But with them, the skeleton that remained also got damp and ultimately disintegrated into the water, in front of my eyes. Frustrated, I killed all the ants which survived the splash, by pressing them against my thumb. I felt good. Sadism, that's the religion I enjoy.

An hour later, to let go of disappointment and frustration, I carefully put all the ants into a sheet of newspaper, together with my shredded memoir, and buried it in the hostel garden, alongside the dahlias. Rest in peace.

In the middle of January, Mr. Singh informed me that editing and typesetting of my work had been completed and it would go into print within a month. One month later, I had two surprises to behold. Tanya was coming back for her semester break, and my book was hopefully going to be out.

I didn't realize how the first month of the New Year passed and February embraced me with its romantic winter. On 2nd February, Tanya wrote a long mail to me, it being our first interaction in the New Year.

Dear Bubu,

I have got two news for you. One is good news, the other is bad news. Since I neither have the time nor the patience to wait for your stupid reply, I'm sharing both of them right now. I'm coming to India for a week, leaving US on 5th Feb, reaching India on 6th morning, 8 am. Mom'll come to receive me. I expect Mom to be a little bit calmer this time, since last week she was very emotional and saying that she was missing me a lot lately. She even said sorry to me for being so brutal to send me away from her. Let's see, I think she is cool about you, and I'm sure that she will be generous enough to let me go out with friends.

The bad news is that the last bit that I wrote is false. My mother absolutely hates you, and it was she who asked Paritosh to be stricter, because you – jackass – once called on my Indian number, didn't you? She asked me whether I was in touch with you, when I assured her that I was no more a crazy girl that I was six months ago. She was absolutely happy.

So by now, I guess, you're smart enough to understand the purpose of this mail. Don't dare call me, or wander anywhere around my home or be found out anywhere I go, because if you do, then my Mom is going to slit your throat or strangulate you. So, DO NOT call me. STAY AWAY from my place. I'll call you as and when I get a chance.

And one more good news, I still love you. See, I'm a spoilt child.

Love.

6ᵗʰ February, 2009

I couldn't sleep that night. I was extremely thrilled. At 6 o' clock in the morning, I went to brush my teeth. When insomnia strikes, this is the best pastime. It gives you a reason why you're awake. My vacant mind suddenly got bombarded with some very intolerable noises, coming from the toilet, fearing the after-effects of which, I immediately rushed out to the verandah. Someone's stomach was in a real bad mood.

I was curious to see who it was. It was Aryan, quite contrary to my presumption that it could be Sameer – *hawa-ka-jhoka.*

'Looks like your stomach had a rough night.' I said, with lather-filled mouth. It sounded like 'loo-lie-you-stoma-ha-a-ro-nai.'

After deciphering what I said, Aryan replied, 'Looks like you have had a rough night.'

'Ah, I couldn't sleep yesterday night.'

'What happened?'

'Tanya is reaching today at 8. I want to meet her but she has advised me strictly to stay away, to avoid any trouble. Her mother would be going to receive her. I'm just anxious, not knowing what to do.' I said, chewing the toothbrush in desperation.

'Come on, you can't just sit here, brushing your crooked teeth while your girlfriend is coming back to the country after 6 long months. Don't be such a spineless dumbass!' Aryan chided me.

'She specifically emailed me not to try anything heroic. She would be very disappointed if I don't agree with her.'

'Dude, stop being such a wimp. Get gutsy and do things that you want.'

'Check her mail. I bet you wouldn't ask me to go if you read it.'

Aryan accompanied me to my room, despite my serious concerns of him polluting my relatively fragrant room.

'She wants you to go to the airport, asshole. If she didn't wish you to come and surprise her at the airport, she wouldn't have informed you. Anyway you wouldn't have known about her arrival, until she told you, didn't you?' Aryan said, his face beaming in excitement.

'Yeah.' His logic seemed flawless to me.

'Let's go then. I'll get the keys of the bike of a senior. Get ready.' Aryan said.

'Are you too coming along?' I asked, astonished.

'If I don't come along, you're not going to reach on time.' Aryan said and rushed to get the keys. Unfortunately, driving motorbikes was not a part of my JEE syllabus and thankfully, for all the needful situations, God had given me Aryan.

'Are you sure, your stomach would let you drive all the way?' I asked Aryan, it being my final question before commencing the awaited journey.

'I need fresh air, and anyway,' He replied, 'it'll be you who would be sitting behind me.'

6.45 am. My sleep was history. I was going to see her. I got ready. Aryan came back with the keys of a Bajaj Pulsar, and said, 'Bajaj will go on Bajaj.'

He kicked off the engine and we vroomed across the campus in a second. It was early morning, traffic had yet not awakened from the hangover of its late night endeavours. He was driving at 110 kmph, my heartbeat was making more noise than the engine. Why shouldn't I be worried? I wasn't even wearing a helmet, a small mistake on Aryan's part and I could be a martyr for the love of my girlfriend. Freezing morning murdered all the romance on my mind.

'When did you learn to drive?' I shouted at the top of my voice.

'A week ago.' Aryan replied from within the helmet. At first I thought I misheard his words. My body was already freezing, but

136

when he said the same thing again, that time my blood froze. I was shivering for two reasons now.

I didn't say a word till we reached the airport. I just held Aryan's waist tightly, as if he was my love interest, and kept on reciting *Hanuman Chalisa* in my mind.

7.50 am. We reached the airport, dashing in the parking space at the speed of 80 kmph. Even the gatekeeper got frightened by Aryan's daredevilry and shouted bad words at us, to which Aryan just showed his most active finger.

We somehow managed to reach the arrival area just in time. The big LCD screen showed that the Air India flight, from New York City to Delhi had arrived. I was very cautious not to encounter my future mother in-law. For that, I had taken out my spectacles, dishevelled my hair and made an oath to myself not to open my mouth. Standing behind Aryan, I gaped at the arrival area. Everything was hazy. Myopia diminished every chance of mine to behold the first sight of my *piya*.

Aryan, who didn't know what Tanya looked like, constantly pestered me with questions like, 'She's hot, right? At least you could tell me which actress she resembles so that I can let you know if I find her. Katrina, Penelope Cruz or Sandra Bullock?'

A sudden commotion at the door induced some activity in my heart as well. The passengers were coming out. I was in an exalted state. I put on my spectacles since I could not afford to miss her.

US returns came out. One by one. Hugs, smiles and laughter

pervaded the atmosphoere around me. Almost fifty people exited, but there was no sign of my beloved. I patiently waited. Aryan, however, was getting impatient.

'I think she has made a fool of you. She is not coming.' Aryan said.

'Wait, I think she's here.' I said, stunned to see the gorgeous. My eyes were stuck at the sight. What a sight! She was wearing a pitch-black one-piece, with red stilettoes, and an immaculate smile. I wanted to run across the hallway and hug her, but I had to be cautious, the reason of my life as well as the prospective cause of my death was around.

She came ahead and looked around. I waited for the lady who sent Ram to Lanka, to bestow her benign presence, but she was not there. I looked here and there, scanned every face present over there, but couldn't find the lady of my nightmares.

Upon not finding my to-be mother in law, I got ecstatic. It was like a dream come true. I jumped like Goofy and rushed towards my beloved. I stealthily merged with the crowd and appeared behind her. I had two choices to surprise her: either by words, or by action. Going by the saying that action speaks louder than words, I spanked her butt. The response that I got was least expected. She turned back and gave one tight slap on my cheek. I was bewildered. I cried, 'Bubu, it's me, Kanav.'

She didn't say a word. But she hit me hard on my legs, with her stilettos. I fell on my knees. It hurt. And then she shouted, 'Get lost! I've nothing to do with you,' and moved ahead.

Action spoke louder than words. I got beaten up in public, by my girlfriend. People around me looked at me with condescending eyes, some of which seemed deadly, as though they would beat me. Before anything could happen, I jumped up and rushed out towards Aryan and immediately, pushed the helmet to cover my face to prevent incitation of any kind of brawl.

'Are you sure that she was the right girl?' Aryan asked.

'Yes, she is my girlfriend. I wouldn't mistake anyone for her.' I said.

'I still doubt. She seemed way out of your league, no offence.' Aryan said, with a devilish smile.

'First it was my girlfriend, and now it's my friend, who's insulting me. Well done.' I said, disgusted.

I was feeling really weird, since despite coming out of the scene of a public assault, I was the centre of attraction for all. After all, I had a helmet on my head. After getting assaulted by a pretty girl, it was the only way to save myself from further fatal beatings by the *aam-aadmi*.

I looked around to have a glimpse of Tanya. She was gone.

'Where did she go? Did you see her?' I asked Aryan.

'Sorry dude. I was busy looking at something more interesting.'

'What was that?'

'*Hamara Bajaj!*' Aryan replied.

We went down to the parking lane, discussing the cause of my assault in public.

'Why did she hit you?'

'I spanked her butt.'

'Oh my God, stud! Are you sure that this is the reason why she had beaten you? Come on, when she had found that it was you, she would not have hit you then. Either she wasn't your Tanya, or else, she doesn't love you anymore.' Aryan said.

'Come on, this is not the case.' I said, trying to convince myself.

'Keep wearing this helmet, I'll show you something.' Aryan said, as he gave the bike a kick-start. 'Hide the number plate with your hand.' Aryan shouted. I did the same. He raced once again through the parking space and went out without giving any fee to the irrascible guard, who couldn't note down the number, courtesy to my acrobatics on the speeding bike.

We moved out of the Indira Gandhi International Airport and fled to the Gurgaon-Delhi expressway. Just when we were halfway, Aryan turned back and said to me, 'Gear yourself up,' and accelerated next to a cab. He maintained a steady speed, and moved along with the car.

When I drifted my eyes towards the car, I was astonished to see a familiar face. Yes, it was beautiful, but at that moment it was scary, since next to it, was the woman of my nightmares. I immediately covered the hood of my helmet, so that no matter what happened I did not come face to face to her or her mother. It was astonishing that she wasn't talking to her mother; despite the fact that she wrote to me that her mother had been missing her.

I kept looking at her from within the helmet, adoring her, not knowing why she had hit me when I was near her, longing her to look at me for once. Suddenly, she turned her head towards us, towards me at first and then towards Aryan. Aryan, with his hair fluttering in the wind, was speeding almost parallel to their cab, unconcerned about the lady in black constantly checking him out.

I felt jealous. I felt cheated. I felt ugly. With a black helmet on my head, I had every reason to feel devastated. Aryan turned back and said, 'What are you waiting for? Say hi to her at least, otherwise she'll continue checking me out.'

I was stunned. Aryan, who I had thought to be a firm believer of the bro-code, was gaping at her from the rear view mirror, all throughout. I pulled over my helmet's hood and stared directly into the eyes of Tanya. I was serious, rather furious. She didn't pay any heed to me. I felt worse than what the ants would have felt when I had crushed them with my thumb. I experienced betrayal, which is worse than death.

I tried distracting her attention, by stretching my hands firstly, then stretching my legs. She remained unfazed. I started playing *tabla* on my helmet.

'What the fuck are you doing? It's making the bike wobble.' Aryan screamed at me. Nevertheless, I continued imitating Zakir Hussain.

Once again, the lady in black remained unfazed. She didn't like Indian classical music, I guess. She liked hot men driving bikes, bloody bitch! I had lost all my hopes from her. A slap in the beginning, checking out another guy for more than five minutes and out-of-this-world sexy outfit, presumably to woo good-looking guys! Could anything be worse? 'For sure, she is cheating on me.' I whispered to myself.

I decided to take my helmet off to get the attention of my girlfriend back. As soon as I reached my helmet, a sudden break halted me. It was my long lost enemy, a policeman on another motorcycle, who became the bottleneck in my pursuit to catch my girl.

'Park your bike on the side.' He ordered.

Aryan followed his order, this time without any finger dancing. I took my helmet off, looking at the cab that I had lost track of. I could see a head hanging out of the back window, looking at us.

'Did she see me? Is she looking at me or Aryan?' I kept thinking, perplexed as never before.

'*Haan bhai*, you people have got hot-blood, isn't it?' The policeman interrupted the train of my thoughts. He had parked his bike alongside, the badge on his white uniform saying 'Suresh Pandey'. He was chewing *paan,* and spoke slightly like Mulayam Singh Yadav.

'Sorry sir.' I mumbled, looking at the cab that went past the horizon.

Aryan pressed my feet with his, silently asking me to shut up and let him tackle.

'Yes sir, may I know why you stopped us?' Aryan charged the police-officer. He stepped back, trying to assimilate the young man's interrogation.

'It was because you weren't wearing any helmet.' The policeman said.

'What if I had been wearing a helmet, would you have stopped me even then?' Aryan continued.

The policeman was really uncomfortable at the ongoing inquiry.

'No.' Mulayam uncle mumbled.

'I know that you would have stopped me even then. I've seen you at work many times, you might not remember me, but when I report your activities to the vigilance commissioner, who happens to be this guy's father,' Aryan pointed at me, 'all your helmet related *nautanki* would go in vain. Kanav, snap Sureshji's picture in your cellphone.'

I was dumbstruck. So was the police officer. How could one lie with such sky-high confidence?

The police officer went back to his bike, kick-started it and went back to his routine job of fleecing from some other biker.

'How could you do that to him?' I asked, shocked.

'Do what? Prevented him from taking a bribe, yes, I feel very sorry.'

'No, you prevented him from taking a genuine fine.' I said, self-righteously.

'Oh, take this bike and rush to give him the "genuine" fine.' Aryan taunted.

I shrugged.

We sped all the way, unable to locate the cab that we had missed.

After getting an early winter morning slap, I didn't dare to go to their place to be strangulated by the deadly mother-daughter duo at the same spot where I once had been brutally assaulted.

I went back to the hostel and slept soundly.

7th February, 2009

I woke up to a phone call. There were twenty-three missed calls already. It reminded me of the good old summer days, I thought I was dreaming and therefore I slept again. The twenty-fourth call shook me up from my slumber.

'You prick! I hate you, I hate you, I hate you.' A familiar voice shouted in US accent.

'You've not seen me yet, how could you hate me? I'm oh-my-God!' I said, purging my drowsiness with raunchy talks.

'Asshole! You're the biggest loser alive.' She shouted. The accent felt as though it was Katrina who was there on the other side of the phone.

'As you say. I know I've lost you. Now tell me whom are you dating?' I asked, seriously.

'He is a biker; I've never seen a more handsome guy before. Yesterday, I saw him on my way back from the airport,' Tanya replied, knowingly or unknowingly raising my temperature, and continued, 'oh yes, airport, that reminds me of what you did yesterday!'

'And that reminds me of what you did to me yesterday.' I said, in a shattered voice.

'You deserved it.' She replied.

'Why? Don't I have any right to spank your butt? Officially, it has been six months since we've been committed and I think, in the progressive world that we live in, it gives me the right to express my feelings at the lack of physical intimacy that we've had. The only thing that we've had since our day of commitment has been those three kisses...'

'Don't remind me of those kisses, it gives me a heart-attack. By the way, it is the cause of your sex-deprived life, you pervert!'

'But why did you slap me and kept kicking me even though you realized that it was me?'

'Had I not slapped you back then this call would not have been possible. I saw that my Mom had just arrived right across the street. If I had not knocked you out, she would have.'

'Oh, still you could have mentioned that your Mom had come.'

'You would have again followed me to display your heroic nature.'

'You know what the entire crowd turned vindictive towards me, I even heard some people shouting catch-that-eve-teaser after me. Had I been caught by the crowd frenzy, I would have been beaten to pulp.'

'I had high hopes that your biker friend would save you. And even if he hadn't, at least he would have been there for me.'

'Jesus! You had already seen us there, hadn't you? And you knew that it was me with the helmet on the bike, right?'

'Yes, duffer. You were the first person I saw in the crowd. Actually, not you but your handsome friend. And, about your bike stunts, I knew that only a person of your stature could do those extremely ridiculous acts on the bike. Even my mother noticed you and called you a lunatic. Thank God you were wearing a helmet and she didn't find out that ugly face behind it. It was so hard for me to control my laughter that I started adoring your driver.'

'Shit! Stop hitting on him. He's already committed.' I said.

'So what? Even I'm.' She said, followed by perhaps a lovely wink, which I didn't want to miss.

'Do you know that a policeman caught both of us?'

'Yeah, it was a moment of relief for me. I just called to inquire whether you are locked up in the jail or somewhere else.'

'I'm at the hostel. Jail does not admit lunatics, you know.'

'Smart. I'll need to get worried now. Since, I know you can't resist coming to meet me.' She said.

'My lady is expecting, ladies and gentlemen, my lady is expecting.' I taunted.

'Funny, in a non-funny way. Douchebag!' She said.

'Tell me something, didn't your mother see me there, when you were assaulting me?' I asked, worried.

'I guess not. The idly eager Delhi crowd gathered around, she couldn't see. But seeing the commotion, she did ask me what had happened to which I replied that I had slapped an eve-teaser.'

'What was her reaction?'

'At first she showed that she was very proud of me, but later she began scolding me for wearing that beautiful one-piece.' She said.

'Oh yes, tell me how was I looking that day?' She continued.

'Hmmm, quite enticing ... for eve-teasers.'

'Jackass!' She squeaked.

'When are we meeting?' I asked the most awaited question at last.

'Oh...mum's here...I...bye bye bye.'

Abrupt ending. She was a master of it. Or a mistress, chuck it. Love knows no grammar.

When I was a child, I used to fantasize a lot about marrying a girl who would be as beautiful as Madhuri Dixit of *Hum Apke Hain Kaun*. Whenever alone in my room, I used to dance to the tunes of *Pehla Pehla Pyaar Hai*, thinking about Madhuri-aunty. Once my mother caught me doing the romantic dance and burst out laughing. I felt so embarrassed that I didn't face her for the next two days. Even to this day, I feel that it has been the most embarrassing moment of my life. Being caught acting romantic by my mother. There is a reason why I am writing all this here. I was scared. Dead scared, since one edited copy of my book had just arrived at my place for proof-reading and I was going through the romantic sequence in my book.

'How would I face my mother?' I contemplated.

'Plus my relatives! All those who had given me the status of the most promising kid of my *khandan*! What would happen when they would read about how well have I lived up to their expectations?' I feared the inevitable, leaving it to time to heal matters.

My parents are cool, but the fear of many of my close relatives, seemed to make me itchy in my bums. An SMS put a stop to my guilt trip.

'Cya at 4 pm, Connaught Place, near PVR Plaza. Bring ample money, we'll party. – Your Bubu' – 8th February, 11.32 am

Just when I started replying back to her SMS, I received a reply.

'Don't you dare reply or call back. This is my Mom's number. And keep those braces at bay else I'll kick you in all the wrong places.'

I smiled. Seeing my smile in the mirror, I decided that it was time to get rid of that wire-frame.

Without wasting any time, I immediately ran to see a dentist, near IIT. He was young, meek and frail. It seemed that he hadn't eaten anything since his childhood. He resembled the kids suffering from kwashiorkor who used to adorn our elementary science books. His clinic seemed like an antique shop, with century old machines, making it look like a haunted house. At the first go, I felt as if I was transported to an earlier century. He had no patients and he eagerly looked at me with his two big eyes protruding out of his face.

Scared, I wanted to run away, but owing to the time crunch, I had no option other than getting treated in hell. I requested him to remove my ugly braces. He didn't agree to my request, saying that I should keep it for another three months at least. I pestered him; he didn't agree and asked me to leave. Annoyed, I stood up from the reclining chair and said firmly, 'My girlfriend is going to kick me in all the wrong places if I go and meet her like this. And if you're not going to remove it, I'm going to kick you in between your legs, right now. If you're ready with the deal, say okay, else keep quiet and I will go and find another dentist.'

He didn't say a word and did his task efficiently, by 2 pm. I looked at the mirror and risked a smile, I was amazed. My smile was what girls would term as cute and charming. No, I'm not boasting, now after writing two books centred on the girl of my life, I have become an expert on female psychology. I felt so grateful to the dentist that I jumped to hug him.

'Please don't! It's against the deal that we had. If you kick me, I'll call the police.' He shrieked.

'Here you go', I said, kissing him on the cheek, while he closed his eyes tightly, in fear of getting hit. I paid his fee and departed.

'I don't ever need to go to a dentist again. EVER.' I felt relieved, hoping that there would never come an occasion when her mother breaks my teeth. I carried a million dollar smile on my face, basking in the glory of my endearing smile.

It was already quarter past 3; fearing Tanya's anger if I reached late, I rushed to the place which witnessed my first daring act – my first proposal. I reached sharply at 4 and waited for around 10 minutes, but there was no sign of Tanya. She had asked me not to call her ever, in Delhi. Ten minutes translated into twenty, my desperation and wait increased with every passing moment. Alas, neither were there any hot chicks around, who could lessen my grave pain.

Finally, a hot chick understood my vexation and called me. My cellphone rang.

'Hey, sorry for the delay.' It was Tanya.

'Oh, you are sensitive, huh.' I said, sarcastically.

'Mom wasn't allowing me to go out initially, but finally I managed. We are going for a movie. Get the tickets done, for the show at 5. We're reaching in 10 minutes.'

'Oh, okay. Corner seats, Ha!' I said, delighted.

'Three tickets please.' She said.

'What!'

'I'm going to bring a friend of mine to the movie.'

'What the hell.' I grieved helplessly.

'She's hot.' She pacified.

'Wow. I will sit in between you two and poke both of you, throughout the movie.' I said.

'Aha! I'll beat you up if you do that.'

'Okay, don't worry. Since you seem to have a problem, I won't poke you.' I said.

'Get lost, jackass.'

'Cya. Pee-ya!'

'You're a bad poet, do you know it?' She rhymed.

'You're a better poet, I know it.' The call was disconnected by then.

I went to buy tickets for the movie. There was no movie at 5. The next movie was at 7 pm. Confused, I turned and forged ahead towards the road, when a scooty screeched to halt just in front of me.

The colour white never looked as beautiful as it was then, right in front of my eyes. She was wearing a white top and a blue capri. Her silky hair was tied into a pony, which jumped up and down as she got down from the pillion. Her eyes seemed to pierce my eyes with the force that they carried. She was looking at me, continuously, without break. Such was the dazzle in front of my eyes that I forgot to even look at the person who was driving. Her lips parted in what could be called as the most seductive smile in this world. There she was, advancing towards me. She wore no make-up, unlike her driver, who seemed to have centrifuged in a tank of foundation cream, eye shadows and what not. Yes, when something as colourful as her driver comes into purview, attention gets diverted from even the best thing around.

'Anjali, meet Kanav.' Tanya said in a typical US accent and clung to my sleeve, slightly pinching my butt, giving my lower half an unconscious twitch. Our palms met and got wrapped in each other. I was holding her hand as tightly as I could. It was colder, softer and firmer than mine. Anjali waved an indifferent hi to me, saying, 'Oh!

So you're the one. I've heard a lot about you.'

'Me too.' I said.

'Wow, I didn't know that you were so famous.' Anjali dug my dumb reply.

'I meant I heard a lot about you.' I said.

'Oh really? I met Tanya on the flight; I wonder how she could talk about me so often? I don't like fakers like you.' Anjali attacked me with her rudeness. She seemed annoyed. I looked helplessly at Tanya, who realized that her friend was doing no good either to me or her.

'Anjali actually, I did talk a lot about you to Kanav. You know, about how you helped me waste my time on buying those worthless dresses at the Dubai airport, about how you behaved like a spoilt child every time you discovered something getting more importance than you, about how you wear those padded bras to make it look like a C when actually you're a B and about how you...' She completely butchered the sarcastic ambitions of her friend, with her immensely exquisite accent, to which I listened with rapt attention. I had all the more reasons to boast about her as my girlfriend.

'Tanya, stop it. We've had enough.' I interrupted, just out of conscience.

'You stop it. I don't know about you but I can't tolerate anyone insulting you in front of me, be it an airplane acquaintance or a close friend. Only I have the right to insult you,' she winked and continued, 'not any dumb bimbo like ...'

Anjali couldn't say anything, she was too dumbfounded. She kick-started her scooty and sped away.

'You didn't need to fight with her.' I said, looking at Tanya,

'Thank me. And thank you. I was looking for a reason to get rid of her for long. I happened to be seated right next to her on the flight and you can imagine how irritable my journey had been. She's the biggest slut that I've ever encountered...'

'Shit! Why the hell did you have to fight with her then! How could you do this to me?' I exclaimed, faking a horrified voice, like the ACP Pradyuman of CID, when he's unable to find a *suraakh* in his pursuit to trace the culprit.

'Ha! Do you need anyone else when I'm with you?' She passed a seductive glance on me and bit her lower lip moving away from me, while our hands still held each other.

'Ahem ahem. I would not mind a threesome.'

She kicked my legs and shouted, 'Jerk!' In return, I patted her back. This time, she reciprocated with a smile. Glad, I patted once again. This time, I got patted back. My bums never felt so happy.

'How am I looking?' I asked, showing my glistening white smile to her.

'Hmm. Pretty...' Tanya mumbled, contemplating.

I interrupted her midway saying, 'Thanks. That's the first time someone called me pretty.'

'I was going to say pretty ugly, as always.' She said with a serious face.

'That's not fair. Please speak the truth.' I said, cracking a devilish smile at her face.

'You always look handsome. You've got a great smile.' She won my heart.

'Do you actually mean it?' I asked, preparing myself for the I-am-touched expression.

'Of course...not. I was just flattering you.'

It seemed that the previous six months of loneliness had just disappeared from my life.

'I have a question.' I said.

'Shoot!'

'How did you know that she was actually a B, not C? Did you see her naked?' I questioned, with my voyeuristic curious face.

'Oh my God, you've become such a pervert. What have you been up to in the last few months?'

'One-man-orchestra. I can give a concert now.' I winked.

'Gross. You are one hell of a sex-deprived pervert.'

'Aren't you? Tell me how did you know that it was padded?'

'She bought half a dozen of those at Dubai Airport. Are you happy now?'

'Yes. Very.' I said, as we strolled around Connaught Circle. 'There were no shows at 5 o' clock. Why the hell did you ask me to book the tickets?'

'I knew, I just said it because that bitch was chewing my brains to book the earliest show.'

Hand in hand, eyes in eyes, deep breaths and simultaneous blinks. We chuckled. We began strolling along the inner circle, passing the showrooms of brands that proved to be a distraction for my beloved. I kept ogling at her and sometimes other girls, while she kept ogling at things and all the time other things. I so desperately wanted to be a Hidesign bag then, when she liked one.

'Ahem ahem. Aren't we supposed to talk?' I said.

'Oh! I'm so sorry. I got carried away.' She said with a guilty smile.

I reciprocated. Just when I opened my newly reconstructed mouth to utter something new, her cellphone buzzed. My moment of togetherness was slaughtered when she said a faint excuse me and picked up the call. I wanted to throw rotten tomatoes at the face of whosoever was on the line. It was her mother. My intention didn't change after the realization, rather it strengthened. Rotten eggs got added to the list.

'No Mom, are you frigging crazy? Why would I see Kanav? I've already told you that I've stopped talking to that scoundrel ever since I went to US.' An Indo-American accent whined assertively.

I was baffled. Seeing the confidence with which she lied to her Mom and the ease with which she called me a scoundrel in front of me, made a shiver run down my spine. I stood there, staring blankly at her, speechless.

'I know. I am no more a fool as I was before, Mom. How can you even think that I would be meeting that dog again? I hate him.'

Now I was a dog. A dog that was hated. What more could I want on my first date after six months?

'I know it's Anjali who bitched about me, isn't it? Well, I just had a fight with her when she was forcing me to go to a pub with her. Never believe her, she is wicked. Yes. Yes. Okay. Yes.'

Bloody slut! Now, all those rotten tomatoes and eggs would be thrown at Anjali. I wanted to cut the tongue of that bitch with a knife. That didn't bring me satisfaction. I now wanted to puncture her scooty as well. Yes, that would have made me feel contented.

'Yes, I didn't go to the pub. Why would I? I'm in Connaught Place. Alone, I was just going to come back.'

Girls. They are excellent liars. I became a huge fan of Tanya. She was such a good liar that she could convince the other person that Justin Bieber is not a girl.

'Mamma, I'm telling you. I'm not with Kanav. Why would I be? I don't even have his phone number. Come here and check yourself. Whatever! You know what, it's really sad the way you suspect me so much. Fine. 10 minutes. Okay, come. Block M.' She said, flustered.

So that was it. 10 minutes of togetherness. That too shared by brands like Esprit, Levis and UCB.

'But before you come, give one tight slap to Anjali. Tell her to get a life.' She said as a parting note to her Mom.

I echoed her feelings, uttering a mild 'yes', when she slapped me hard on my cheek.

'Why the hell did you have to open your mouth?' Tanya thundered.

I couldn't answer. Since I was bad at coming up with lies, I stuck with the truth. 'It was instantaneous.'

'Great. Now instantaneously, get going. My mother is near CP, she is going to arrive here in just 5 minutes.' She said.

'Can I get a hug?' I pleaded, submissively.

'Only if you dare.' She said with a smile. We hugged. Not long. Rather short and sweet.

'When are we completing this incomplete date?' I asked.

'Tomorrow. Same place. Same time.' She was quick with her reply.

'Ass, you like it.' I said, pointing at her back.

'Jackass!' She exclaimed.

'Bye. You're a great liar. This dog wishes that someday we'll lie together, in each other's arms.' I said and retraced my steps farther, farther until a bunch of bigheads hid her from my sight.

9th February, 2009

The next day took a lot of time to arrive. It was difficult passing every moment. The hands of the clock took a lot of time to move even by a millimetre. To kill the irreprissible wait, I attended lectures after a long time and listened to what my professor was teaching. His talk seemed interesting.

It was mechanics. He was talking about a guy, who was sitting in an aeroplane, and suddenly he discovered this innate urge to start skipping on the plane. And that's not the end of the story – even his skipping increased its speed with every passing moment. And now our dear professor posed a 'problem', which he said to be very interesting, that he wanted us to calculate the speed of a car moving on earth relative to that rope. What a problem! I thought. I solved it first and shouted my answer in the class, to which my professor gave a delighted smile, which was in a subtle contrast to his serious face.

The moment the classes got over, I rushed to the same place where I had been referred to as a dog and a hated scoundrel to meet the same person who labelled me with those special words, in the hope of getting some more compliments that day.

She was there, this time before me, in the same dress that she had worn the day before, which is quite unexpected in the case of girls.

'So, it seems that somebody has not taken a bath.' I greeted her with a taunt.

'It seems somebody has been noticing me too much.' She said. And thus we began our conversation. The previous day, she had convinced her mother that I was no more than a dark spot of her past and she was over me. She related to me how much she hated lying to her mother, but at the same time she said that she wouldn't be lying to her had her mother ever agreed to listen patiently to what she had to say. I was touched, saddened at first and gladdened later on. Saddened because I couldn't help her in any way and gladdened because she made me feel really valued.

How the next three hours went, only God could tell. We talked about everything in this world, everything of our world and everything of the other world where she used to live. There was not a single moment when our eyes drifted from each others. Such was the magnetism of the moment, that even when I blinked my eyes, I could see her eyes. Romance, when sprinkled with longing, becomes a delicacy worth treasuring.

'I'm strictly against public display of affection.' I said, out of the blue, feeling a bit uncomfortable on seeing a couple doing some twisting and untwisting in the nearby seat.

'And I am strictly against your opinion.' Tanya said, hugging me suddenly.

'Well, I just realized that it ain't that bad.' I said, stunned. 'What - your opinion or PDAs?'

'My opinion. If my opinion attracts a hug, it's worth keeping it.'

Hand in hand, we sat at our very own place, where I had once proposed to her. Barista. We replayed the scrabble proposal; she decided that we would swap roles. I became the earlier Tanya and she played the earlier me. I enacted the dead look that she had on her face the moment I mumbled 'I love you too' to her, and walked away swaying my bums at her face, making her realize how I felt when she had done the same to me.

Every relationship becomes special through such memories scattered throughout the sands of space and time. If given the opportunity, I would buy the same place and make it into my living room.

Having found her daughter at home after six months, her mother had become a little lenient. Tanya left her home on the pretext of meeting her school friends and she had to return before 9. Thankfully, our sanity prevented us from getting carried away towards crossing the time limit.

'Time to leave.' She said.

'Time flies, when I'm with you.' I mentioned.

She smiled.

'No time for cheese. Good bye.' She said, giving me a short hug.

'Good bye without a kiss is like a ...' I started thinking for a suitable simile until it dawned to me, 'superman without underwear.'

'No,' a strict reply followed.

'What now, there ain't any braces this time! Why not?' I pleaded.

'If the smile had been a little better, I would have given it a thought.' She taunted and moved ahead, towards the metro station gate.

'*Acha*, as you wish. Wait a minute, I've to tell you something.'

'What?' She screamed from three yards away.

'Come here, it's something personal.' I said, making a mysterious face.

'What? Come on, I'm getting late.' She uttered, irritably.

'Come near, I'll whisper. It's personal.' I said. She was curious, her face telling me the entire story. I went near her left ear, and whispered in a scared voice; 'You know what!' and I kissed her cheek.

'Asshole!' She shouted as I ran away from her, towards the staircase.

'I'm not coming from there. Bye, you cheat.' She said and trudged towards the elevator.

I ran across the pavement and joined her in the elevator. I was panting, she was breathing deeply. There was a big mirror on the other side. I looked at her image in the mirror, which was accidentally looking at me. The door closed. It was just the two of us, and our images. I kept looking at her reflection, which suddenly pounced on me. We hugged, we kissed and we almost ate each others' face. Her fragrance, the smell that had not allowed me to sleep for months, captivated my mind once again.

'Bubu, I love you so much.' She whispered, to which I dumbly nodded. She was in my arms, I was in hers. If there could be one thing that I would have wished at that moment, it would have been to stop time at the point.

Suddenly, Tanya pushed me away, while I didn't let go. I didn't know what happened, for my closed eyes were too busy living in the world of my beloved. When I opened my eyes, I saw a frail old lady looking at us from right outside the elevator. The elevator door opened and as a matter of fact, we had forgotten to push the down button. Embarrassed, I pushed the close door button again and again, but it didn't work, since the old grandma had a jutebag placed on the door. I pulled Tanya's hand and both of us vanished from the elevator in a moment, without giving any more mild heart attacks to the old lady.

'Ultimately, it's the staircase that came to rescue.' I said. Tanya was numb, as if she'd seen a ghost.

'She was my grandma.' Tanya said, appalled.

'OMG. Really? Do your relatives keep spying on you?' I joked.

'She died five years ago.' She whispered.

I experienced a sudden shiver. I was horrified. My tongue became parched. Now, God was sending ghosts after me. What more could be wrong in my life!

'Good bye,' Tanya said like a robot, as she moved towards the security check at the metro entry. I stood still, seeing her disappear in the crowd. My cellphone vibrated.

'Bubu, I was kidding. Now change your expression.' The SMS read.

I had been fooled, for good. She was gone. And I had nothing but to smile at the ordeal we'd just faced.

'We should have continued kissing further. She would have gone back to where she belonged.' I messaged her back. The date was over. The feeling remained.

The next two days were spent in the bed of words. SMSes, the romantic, sentimental, emotional and most importantly, the naughty ones, were in the air. My fingers became so adept in typing messages that I could have written another book on the cellphone itself.

To elaborate, Tanya had got a cellphone and her mother seemed to have become less careful about her 'careless' daughter, thinking that Paritosh's rigorous guardianship and her motherly animosity might have kicked out any kind of love that was there inside her little head.

However they didn't realize that she carried the same genes of rigidity as her mother. The girl of my dreams never allowed me to dream in the two days that followed our first meeting. She would call me from within the loo, whispering innately romantic poems that she had written for me while she was away, followed by the dulcet noises of running water, brushing teeth and sometimes, even … okay, I was going to exaggerate! It's not cool visualising a beautiful girl making music in the loo.

Even buying an SMS pack of five hundred SMSes daily seemed to be too few to say what we had to say to each other. I loved my love story, so much so that I started caring more about us than ever before. It was very hard for me to resist sharing with her about my novel.

'It's going to be the best surprise ever possible.' I kept reminding myself.

Not to forget to mention that my academics were flushed down in the drain, together with every toilet conversation that we've had. Thanks to my literary pursuits and perpetual excitement about the woman of my life, I had decided not to bestow my benign presence to my dear professors. I was not very fond of seeing them, since I would not be listening to them anyway. Not because I would be daydreaming about someone far more good-looking than them, but because I would be 'dreaming' about the same.

'When are we meeting next?' I asked Tanya, who was once again busy fighting with the mosquitoes of Delhi in the loo, on 8th February, after my adept fingers got tired of typing and my newly found mouth wanted to start a never-ending conversation. She was finding it difficult to find time to move out since her mother had called some of her very distant relatives at her place, and she had to entertain them, almost all the time.

'12th February.'

'What's on 12th?'

'It's Ruchi's birthday, jerk. Don't you remember?'

'Of course.' I said, faking about the almost forgotten birthday that once shaped my love life.

'You're bad with dates, both kinds. I'm thoroughly disappointed.'

'But, I'm good with tits, both kinds.'

'Wannabe.' She remarked, in her distorted Indo-US accent. *Dilli-ki-hawa* had its effect on her tongue.

'Yes, I want to be those.' I uttered. She would have blushed on the other side of phone, I could see it.

'Great. I can see where are you going, the next porn star!' She whispered.

'*Beta*, is there someone inside?' A voice struck my ears.

'Oh ma, it's just me. I was humming.' Tanya replied, before the call dropped.

'How about a guided IIT tour by yours truly, on 11th? After the tour, we'll watch your favourite movie together on my laptop.' I messaged her. I couldn't wait

'No.' She replied. The word upset my mood.

'Did I say no? Actually, I meant yes. I can't resist meeting your hot biker friend!' She made my night.

Dear Kanav,

The first edition of your book has gone into printing. We expect the first two thousand copies to reach us by 12th February. We have a tradition at our publishing house that the first bundle of the books is unpacked by the author, to let him hold his creation before anybody from our office does. It brings us great pleasure to invite you to our office on 12th morning, at around 11 am, to receive the first bundle of books with your hand.

Regards,
Anirudh Singh
Karma Publishers

Drop after drop trickled down my face. I could not believe what was happening. It was like the entire universe was conspiring to fit everything in place, much like what I had once expected. I was touched by the lovely gesture shown by my publisher.

I was checking my email after two days and the mail proved to be an icing on the cake. 12th February! Come on, in the entire universe, nothing could have been a better co-incidence. I was going to meet her for the one last time, before she left for the States for God knows how long, and I was going to have my book in my hand; 'our' book in her hand.

I could not stop visualizing the smile, the amazement on her face, the slight shiver of joy and irresistible hug that I would be gifted when I would give her the grand surprise.

Guide to Galaxy Aphrodisia

Can you expect me to hide my excitement from her for the next four days? It was tough, but I did it. Courtesy my SMS packs. I kept her involved, in random stuff that I fabricated during my classes, gaining negative inspiration from my professors, thinking that if I pay attention in the class, I might turn out to be like one of those. Not that they were bad or ill-tempered, but most of them were as boring as their faces depicted them to be.

One original message that I clearly remember read:

A proposal, if accepted, makes it love.

A proposal, if rejected, makes it infatuation.

A proposal, if not dared, makes it desperation.

A proposal, if it scared, makes it mortification.

This was the first small creation that she replied with a 'wow' and she continued, 'so you've finally managed to become a poet.'

Talking about the SMSs, I've had a plenty of interesting SMS conversations, with her, which I'm skimming through right now in my cellphone. Ah, here I find one.

Tanya: What do you think of long distance relationship?

*I: It can work, if the girl agrees to pay all the telephone bills. *wink**

Tired of always being the first one to be creative for her, I pestered her to write a poem for me, but unfortunately, I got digged myself.

I: Will you write a poem for me?

Tanya: Sure. But, I'm not too sure whether it would be good.

I: Why are you saying so? You're good, I know.

Tanya: I've never mocked people in my poems before.

I: You're bad, you know.

Things couldn't get more brutal, with her sarcasm mocking me every time we had a conversation. Her naughty streak continued, as she kept enlivening my moments, with her sharp comments and slapstick humour.

Tanya: What are your friends like?

I: They're people who you would never like.

Tanya: Oh, simply tell me that they're like you. And, you're so right about the liking part.

Recently, Anuj, while going through my messages of that time, without my permission, took out the best conversations that I have had with Tanya, and compiled them. When I caught him intruding my privacy, he immediately jumped on my feet and cried, 'Gurudev, this was what I was looking for. Hot girls like sharp replies! This is going to be my "Guide to Galaxy Aphrodisia". And I've not read any of those messages with *bubus* written in them, though I desperately wanted to.'

'Asshole,' I shouted as he ran away.

'Do share these in your next book. You're going to help many more *bubus*!' He shouted as he ran away.

To expose the reality of Anuj Roy, the wit-master par excellence, as thought by her current date, I think I should better share some of the key topics of the 'Guide to Galaxy Aphrodisia', as he calls it.

Tanya: In love, you can make no mistakes.

I: Wrong!

Tanya: That was the best way to define love. What was wrong in that?

I: In love, you can make one mistake every nine months.

Tanya: OMG, you're such a cheese-bag!

I learnt her skill as fast as I could and gave her tough competition.

I: What does your Mom think about me?

Tanya: She thinks you to be a wicked rascal and a repugnant prick.

I: Would you do me a favour?

Tanya(concerned): Sure. Did you feel bad?

I: A little bit, for her spoilt daughter, for she's been dating this wicked rascal and repugnant prick since the last one year. Now, did you feel bad?

Tanya: Wicked rascal!

See, ain't I good?

Tanya: It's very difficult to find the right guy.

I: It's even more difficult to find the 'wrong' girl!

Tanya: What do you mean?

I: Ah, it's simple. To a guy, every second girl seems to be the right one - the perfect match! But, be rest assured because I'm not that type.

Tanya: Thanks for letting me know that you're not a guy. Now, I'm rest assured. Jerk!

Ironically, during that period, Tanya talked about my novel as well, but she didn't mean it seriously. Do you remember, that I had used this tactic to once woo her?

Tanya: You said that you were going to write a novel. Was it really true or were you just trying to impress me?

I: Wasn't it a novel way to impress you?

Tanya: Oh yeah, "quiet" novel!

I: Sometimes, I wish to be in that age where there was no phone, no emails, but just a handwritten letter as a mean to convey one's longing for the loved one residing far away.

Tanya: Sometimes, I wish to hold that handwritten letter. The Indian postal service still functions, in case you didn't know.

No point in guessing, she's smarter than me, at times.

Tanya: Why are boys so crazy about getting a girl's phone number? The girls anyway aren't going to entertain them.

I: Some girls do entertain such guys.

Tanya: Oh, only the dumb ones would fall in such a trap.

I: Don't say that. My girlfriend would be offended.

But I'm smarter, most of the times. Since it's my book, I'll make sure that I'll present a balanced point of view i.e. biased towards me.

I: Many a times, I wonder how such a pretty girl like you could fall for me?

Tanya: Because we're so similar.

I: How can you say that?

Tanya: Because many a times we think exactly the same thing!

This time, she totally nailed it. We were messaging each other at 2 at night. I screamed such a loud 'F word' in amazement after getting what she meant; it woke almost all my neighbours.

Tanya: What did you miss all the while you were away?

I: I missed my heart.

Tanya: Cute.

I: You know why I missed it? I gave it to so many girls all along. Now say cute!

Tanya: Huh. Jackass!

Guys like me, who've never ever got any attention from the fairer sex before, have this tendency to brag about the imaginary possession of so many girls we have dated. Our imagination is pretty strong. Girls take it as perversion, however. It's not our fault, you see, if they can't see the good side.

I: You're the most important thing in my life.

Tanya: Thanks. I had never been acknowledged for being the most important 'thing' in somebody's life.

I: Don't feel bad. Things change, you know.

Thank you thank you, you can compliment me by writing a mail. She didn't have any answer for it.

I: Will you marry me?

Tanya: Not even in your dreams.

I: It's okay. Marry me in your dreams.

Tanya: In your dreams!

*I: That's what I said. *wink**

I would not brag now. I'm practising modesty. By the way did you see how awesome I was?

The next conversation, it's like the Wit God speaking from within me. And girls, I'm modest.

I: Six days a week, I think about you.

Tanya: But what about the seventh day?

I: The seventh day I flatter you with such beautifully crafted lies.

Tanya: Huh. Jerk!

To make the game even, I am giving my able competitor a chance to show her talent, in proving me dumb. I surrender, for her.

I: Of all the things women possess, intellect appeals the most to me. Rarity charms, you know!

Tanya: Opposites attract, you know!

I: All the girls in my life have been dumb.

Tanya: Oh! That tells me how they could stand you.

On marriage:

I: Will you marry me, if I agree to dispose of your husband?

Tanya: Yes, but I would need your help again.

On love at first Sight:

Tanya: Do you know what the first thing that I noticed in you was?

I: My wit?

Tanya: No. Your face.

I: Did you find me handsome?

Tanya: No, I found you ugly. And then, found you boring as well.

I: What made you hook up with me then?

Tanya: Your misconception!

I think we've had enough of appreciation for the young lady. Let me finish off the Guide to Galaxy Aphrodisia, with the last bit where I, modestly, emerge to be better than the lady of the hour.

Tanya: Some days you make me feel on the top of the world.

I: When would you make me feel that, my world?

Now that I've proven my supremacy, I would like to share the most integral element of the Guide to Galaxy Aphrodisia. I once asked Anuj, what he meant by love. His reply was classic:

Love means being able to flatter your girlfriend so well that even if she finds you having a fling with her roommate, she would go to her instead and yell, 'Bitch. Leave my guy.'

I just wish that Anuj's current girlfriend goes through his description about love in this book and realizes what piece of shit she is dating. Don't you wish the same?

Interestingly, I asked my dear lady the same question. Her answer could melt anybody's heart, except people like – oh chuck it, it's not nice to bring your mother-in-law everywhere. Here goes her reply:

LOVE: 'I say, he listens. He says, I listen. Both say, none listen. None say, both listen. That's love.'

Anuj, after reading Tanya's definition of love, impressed five girls on Facebook for a date with him. To all the habitual stalkers reading this book, here's the thing you'd been looking for! Leave this book and explore the trick. If it doesn't pay you back in kind, sue Anuj. Contact me for his address.

3. The End

I ain't a superman, but if I could fly, I would not have worn underwear above my pants, no matter how sexy the underwear might have looked. It was 11th February, 2011. It's not about undies or burgundies; it's neither about Anuj, Sameer nor Aryan, nor is it about me and my beloved. It's about Superman, who returned. I had elaborately laid a plan, where Tanya was supposed to come to IIT, for the very first time in her life and we were to watch Superman Returns, just because she was a huge fan of Superman.

How could any girl like a muscular hunk wearing an underwear, that too a red one over tight blue pants? And didn't Superman feel embarrassed showing his big calves in those tight pants? Bloody gay! Must have a teeny weeny.

Anyhow, so here I was, in IIT, prepared to miss all my classes including a very important practical, just because I had given her my word that I would be giving her a guided tour of my alma mater. I was waiting for my dear lady to grace the venue with her elegant footsteps. She had asked me not to call her, since her mother would be dropping her to Saket, from where she would be taking an auto to IIT.

I waited. Eagerly at first, painlessly later on, helplessly when painlessness turned into helplessnesss. She didn't come. It started with ten minutes, and went up to 2 hours. I dared to call her two times in between. She cut the phone. I controlled my vexation.

My entire wait seemed to have been worthless. However there was one thing that soothed my heart. I didn't have to watch a handsome guy wearing red underwear over his tight pants showcasing his huge calves to none other than my girlfriend.

Lost in thoughts of superman, Tanya, underwears and butts, I strolled back to my hostel, carrying the heavy laptop bag. I dragged my sagging body up the stairs to the top floor, where my little messy *hut* was situated. I had missed all my classes, two of which I could have easily attended had I not wasted my time in waiting for her. Just when I dropped the heavy laptop on the bed, heaving a loud sigh of disappointment, my phone rang. It was Tanya. It was the first time in my life that I got pissed seeing her name on my phone-screen.

'What the fuck do you want? Where have you been?' I shouted.

'Hey, I'm really sorry. My Mom changed her plan and she didn't drop me at Saket, instead she took me to meet some friend of hers.'

The intensity of my irritation peaked and the volcano of anger erupted.

'Fuck you and your…,' I uttered and realized what had come out of my mouth. 'Anyway, where are you now?' I tried to maneouvre my earlier words. But she wasn't someone who could be easily dodged.

'Do you realize what you said just now? You've lost all the respect in my eyes.' Tanya said harshly, in a hurt voice.

'What? I've just asked you where you are now, what's wrong with that?' I said, defiantly.

'Well, now lie openly. I didn't expect to hear, never ever, what you had just said to me.'

'What? I just said "fuck you", that was just a friendly remark, lovers do make love, don't they?' I humoured her a bit. She was unmoved.

'It wasn't about your first exclamation, but what followed it. You know what I'm talking about. How dare you say that?' She thundered.

'Tanya, listen to me. Tanya, please. I wasn't going to …' I said.

'I had arrived in your campus, but now I think I had better go. I feel disgusted with you.' Tanya said and disconnected the phone.

I was flabbergasted. Dumbstruck. 'What the f…, hell!' I exclaimed, checking my natural proclivity towards the F word. I called her back, it was switched off.

I remained standing in my room, blankly staring at the wall. I looked at my phone and couldn't conceive of doing anything that could repair the last three minutes that I'd spent. I looked at the watch and suddenly a shiver of guilt ran across me.

I started running. I jumped the stairs in record time, four at a time, dashed out of my hostel and hurried towards the main gate. Sometimes, love requires you to run an extra mile; it was my sometime. I ran, ran and ran. Stray dogs, on the way, found me an interesting character and started racing along with me, until I realized that they were after me. I exerted more, endured more and beat them in their own race.

My eyes scanned each and every nook and corner that I could see to find my beloved. She wasn't here. She wasn't there. Nowhere.

I was panting; my t-shirt was already soaked in what seemed like a mixture of my sweat and pee. I couldn't see, sweat from my forehead inundated my eyeballs and made me partially blind. There was a thick layer of moisture on my glasses. I couldn't see clearly. My helplessness vexed me more than ever before and not finding Tanya made no sense to me since all my hardwork didn't deserve to go unrewarded. That's what I thought.

I called her once again, this time she picked up.

'Where are you? Please don't go.' I said, trying to overcome my panting.

'I'm leaving, don't try to find me. I don't want to meet you.' She rebuked.

'Please listen to me. I didn't mean to say what I said…' I said, still struggling with my breath. My sweat made it impossible to hear what she was saying. It seemed that my ear was also clogged with it.

'Hey, please tell me where you are…' I urged, for the very last time, this time shouting at the top of my voice. She disconnected the call without saying a thing. I was completely flustered. I decided to call her once again, her behaviour was not only undesirable but actually, irritable. She couldn't be unjust to me just for a lame cause.

I dialled her number. It turned out to be busy. I had lost my mind. Making a mess out of my life, she had decided to have a chit-chat with some bloody lunatic she had in her family. A moment later, 'Tanya calling' was what I encountered in my phone screen. Seeing her name drove me mad, this time.

I picked up the phone, and without even listening to what she was saying to me, I began my enraged monologue.

'What the fuck do you think of yourself? That you could do anything to me and go away? You're no more than an average loser stuck in my life from nowhere.'

'Kanav, please…' Tanya said.

If given a chance, I would permanently erase those twenty seconds from my life. It was the first time not only she had come across my dark mercurial side, but it was a surprise for me as well. And the story didn't stop there, I continued being bitter for another minute.

'Shut the fuck up. I'm tired of listening to you. You listen to me. What do you think? I don't feel bad? You're the biggest mistake of my life. I repent every second that I've spent in your memory. But not anymore. Get out of my life. Go and live in hell with your insane family, consisting of all the bunch of pricks.' I said, with broken breaths.

'Kanav, please … I just called you to say that I'm standing right behind you, but I guess I shouldn't have stayed after seeing you here. I am feeling...' She cried on the phone, disconnected it and continued from behind me, 'terrible. Thanks for everything.'

She was sobbing. Her face looked like a child's whose favourite toy had just got stolen. I felt nothing. I was taken aback at what had just happened. It seemed that all the love that existed between us had been blown by my hateful words. I was not feeling anything.

'Hey, please don't cry.' I mumbled insincerely and consciously extended my hand to her face, trying to wipe the drops that I'd been seeing from such a close range for the first time. She pushed my hand away. Each and every drop on her face seemed like a hard slap on my face, harder than what was gifted by her mother long ago. It hurt me, despite the fact that I was still very rigid about how annoyed I felt at her resentment with me over what I felt was a trivial issue.

'Please don't cry. People know me here, if they see you crying, no girl would ever consider me for an assault.' I humoured, to chill her mood. She wasn't in the mood to get calmer.

'Hey, wait,' I said, seeing her stumble towards the main gate, 'don't you think you're overreacting for just a silly cause?' I asked.

'It's not a silly cause. There should be a limit to everything. You can't go on saying anything that you want. How dare you say anything about my mother?'

'What? Oh, you're still angry about that! I was going to say, 'fuck you and your mother's friend,' it was not what you think.' I lied, openly.

'That's what you're good at – resorting to lies to save your soul. You know what, I hate you.' She winced, irritably, making a how-could-you look on her face. I walked behind her, having no idea what to do.

Suddenly she stopped, turned back and shrieked, 'Initially, I felt offended when you abused me and my mother because I didn't expect that from you, not even in my wildest dreams. But now I'm not feeling bad because I've no feelings left for you. I just realized that you were never the person I thought you were. Thanks for showing your real self, full of hatred, disrespect and lies.'

Pearl shaped drops were trickling down her eyes, down her cheeks. We had become a centre of attraction for people nearby, a majority of them being desperate lecherous engineers and some of them curious fat aunties rapid-walking to trim their bodies. I tried to shoo them away by a mere rebuke but they didn't seem to listen. I concentrated on Tanya again, when I realized that she had already started walking towards the main gate.

'Please don't go.' I caught her hand from behind and said, 'I love you.' It was the most insincere I love you ever.

'Don't ever dare to say that to me again.' Tanya said seriously. She was terribly pissed.

'I told you that I didn't mean it that way. I said whatever I could.' I averred.

'Except sorry.' Those were her last words, that day, which echoed in my head forever.

A bus suddenly came and took her away from me. I couldn't feel anything. I watched her disappear right in front of my eyes. Even Superman couldn't have saved me from the disaster that had just happened.

I walked back to my hostel room hoping that things would get better as her mood got better. Anger and grief fades away with time. But, not love, I hoped.

A kilometre long introspective walk from the main gate back to my hostel brought me back to my senses. With every step that I trudged, it seemed as though a heavy brick of guilt was put over my heart. By the time I reached my hostel, the burden on my heart had become so heavy that I had difficulty in walking. I was dragging myself all along.

There is a difference between being deplorable and being shattered. Betrayal shatters you but it is guilt that makes you deplorable. In the case of betrayal, it makes you question, 'why did I trust him/her?' while in case of guilt, it makes you question yourself, 'why was I ever born?' or 'why couldn't I die before that happened?'

I was withered. I was deplorable. I was every bloody adjective which was synonymous with the word crushed, except 'squeezed'.

Upon deep reflection, I just couldn't believe what I had just become in front of Tanya. I was sorry. I wanted to tell her the same. I wanted to say sorry to her, a million times, maybe a zillion times, not just because I wanted to win her heart back but because I was actually apologetic. I would have smashed the face of the person who could dare abuse my family members. I called her. Her cell-phone was switched off.

For the next six hours, I messaged numerous 'sorry' messages to her, but alas, no reply. I wondered whether she received them or not. I tried every fix possible, but it was not reciprocated, not even in the negative way.

It was a cold night. My heart seemed frozen, looking for warmth that it had just lost. I lay on my bed, crouched like a baby around the pillow, holding it tightly against my chest for what seemed like moral support. The date had crossed. It was Ruchi's birthday. I didn't feel like wishing her at the stroke of midnight, I was just not in the right mood. I lay on my bed, unconcerned about how darkness embraced with dawn, constantly looking at my cellphone to no response.

'I'm going to meet Tanya tonight at Ruchi's party. I'll fix everything there. After all, I'll have my book to surprise her with.' I said to myself. Thinking about the book, I replayed the entire sequence mentioned in the book and was very glad to realize that I hadn't written anything offensive about her mother, from Tanya's perspective.

'I'm not a bad guy. It's the anger that made me one.' I pacified myself for my action the day before.

The insomnia diluted my early morning thoughts and I slept for around three hours. It was another day. The day of the book and the beloved! I went to my publisher and collected the very first copy of my book. The moment when he handed me over a lot to cut and inaugurate made me feel on the top of the world. I wished Tanya had been around. I was perpetually smiling. My sleepy eyes were dazed in the thrill of holding my own child in my hands. I flipped through the pages, the pages which contained the thrill of my first conversation with Tanya, our first hand holding, our first hug and our very first kiss. Mr. Singh asked me to gift him a signed copy, which I gleefully did. I wrote, 'Thanks for making my dream come true.'

Excitedly, I came back to my place, holding the six complimentary copies that I had got. I snapped a dozen of photographs of them. I tried her number, it was switched off. I got a bit ruffled, but still was dazzled by the excitement of what I was holding in my hand.

An hour later, I called Ruchi, saying, 'So, where's the party tonight?'

'Waikiki, just for you guys.' She said.

'That's so sweet of you. Did you speak to Tanya?' I asked.

'No, I did not. I was expecting her call since midnight. Is she fine?' She asked.

'Oh yes, she must be. She might be busy preparing some gift for you. By the way, I'm going to bring a very special gift for you. I hope you love it.' I said.

'Well, well, sure. I'm waiting. Cya.'

'Yes, cya. And by the way, let me think, I had to say something that I'm forgetting. Oh yeah, *Mubaraka* for the birthday!'

'Huh, better late than never. By the way, your better half is calling right now, so I better take your leave. Looking forward to your special gift, hope it outshines what your Tanya brings!' She said.

So she was alive. And she was in her senses. A big, stupid smile cracked open on my face. I was eager to cast a spell on my lady.

I continued messaging her and trying her number. She was not reachable. I called her at the landline but unfortunately, my *jaani-dushman* picked up my call a couple of times. Every time I heard her voice, a huge weight of guilt mounted on my heart. Before giving up, I tried the landline number for the one last time. Luckily, this time it was Tanya who picked up.

'Hello.' Tanya said from the other side. I could feel her breaths from miles away.

'Hi Bubu, please listen to me. I'm really really sorry for whatever I said. I would never do it again.'

'Listen, I am telling you for the very last time. I'm nobody to you. It's better if you leave me to my own destiny.'

'I'm sorry. I love you.'

'Thank you. I don't believe that and neither do I appreciate that. If you really do mean what you say, please stay away from me.'

'Please listen to me. I'll fix everything tonight, at Ruchi's birthday,

I promise. I'm sorry. I mean it.'

'Ma, someone wants to talk to you, he's been constantly saying sorry for something.' She said.

Frightened, I disconnected in no time. I didn't have the courage to die young. I was anyway going to meet her in the evening, I consoled myself.

I was getting ready for Ruchi's birthday party. I took out the best of clothes that I had after all I was going to steal her show, with my rare gift to her. It was after a long time that I had spent so much time in front of the mirror. I made sure that I had attended to all the *prakriti* calls that I had to, made sure that it was not the toothpaste that I shaved with and sprayed one full bottle of musk on my favorite shirt, only a moment later to repent at what I had done.

Tanya was allergic to musk – which meant that either I had to let go of my favourite shirt or to let go of her. I choose the prior. I could not let her go yet another time. And also, I couldn't stand her streak of 'aaaahcheee's, which though sounded cute, but could be avoided. I had a mission to fulfill, to win back the heart of my beloved. I changed my shirt to a 'sober' T-shirt adorned with a skeleton holding another skull. It was gifted to me by one of my sisters, who mentioned, 'from now on there will be something more dreadful than your serious face.'

'What if she doesn't forgive?' I questioned myself. It was a serious question, since I noticed a grave look on my shining face. The intricate pattern of wrinkles on my forehead clearly showed that I was being tortured by a girl.

I got an idea – an idea, which instantly transported me from the gloomy world to the world of happiness. It was my saviour for the night. If the beautiful lady doesn't seem to be in a mood to accept my plea, I would kneel down and gather the support of everyone. She doesn't like the limelight and would eventually consider my request. Girls like guys surrendering in front of them, don't they? Don't you remember the temple incident of my debut novel?

Anyway, I was getting late and it was time to move on to enchant my enchantress. I gift-wrapped two books of mine, one for the lady with the birthday and other for the lady with my everyday. On the first book, I wrote, 'Thanks for being born. If it hadn't been you, you wouldn't be holding this gift in your hand (pun intended!). A very happy birthday to the person who made this book possible!' I signed it. It was the first time my signature was no more a signature. It was an autograph.

Thinking what to come up for the second book made my heart tremble a bit. Should I apologize, or should I propose, or should I just speak my heart out?

Confused, I stole the lines from my very own book and scribbled them on the front page.

Oh little star!
Will you take my wish to her who is so far
Tell her that I am
Just a little lonely here...
I had never known that practicising my signature would come to
my use someday. With love, Kanav

Laughing at what I thought as my ingenuity, I gift wrapped both of them immediately without noticing which one was which. Once I realized my mistake, laughing at my stupidity, I unwrapped both of them. The book with its bright blue cover looked more enticing that the gift wrapped ones. I wrapped them in a newspaper, just for the element of surprise, put them in my bag and embarked my journey to replay the role that I had played a year ago, in a much better way.

It was the same. Exactly the same. The setting, the balloons, the lights and the cake. Ruchi had made sure that not only the restaurant but the entire setting should be exactly the same as the previous time, as desired by us. She was standing right at the elevated step, receiving the gifts from her friends one by one, as she was a year ago.

As soon as I moved ahead, the background music changed to a popular number and people started dancing all throughout. Ruchi, fortunately saw me in the process, and came forward and held my hands taking me to the dance floor. If there is something that I'm exceptionally talented in, it is bad dancing.

'Happy birthday, birthday girl.' I said, a bit consciously since I was holding her waist for the very first time.

'Thank you, honeypie. Move your feet, move your feet. Dance on the rhythm. Follow me.' She was in another mood, probably a little intoxicated or just super-excited. She revolved round, danced like a queen and made me feel even more conscious. My legs were trying to imitate whatever she was upto; my body was stiff and my eyes drifted around to find the lady, for whom the atmosphere had been specially set. I couldn't find her.

In the meanwhile, I did notice something. There was a little addition from the last time. There was a wine table in the corner. I got the reason behind the new avatar of Ruchi.

'Wow, you dance so well,' I complimented, 'looks like *ache se chadhi hai!*

'Nothing hides grief better than vodka, isn't it?'

'Indeed!' I said. 'By the way, how come the birthday girl is unhappy?'

'Two reasons.' She said while dancing and heavily breathing.

'One, my best friend isn't coming to the party and second, all my efforts to make it the best reunion for you two has gone awry.'

A slap of realization hit me hard on my face.

'Are you talking about Tanya?' I confirmed. She nodded, while dancing.

Suddenly, my feet got stiff and I no more moved on the dance floor. Ruchi, a little bit high, kept dancing and didn't let go of my hand. She tried to drag me but I detached my hand from hers, and moved away. I was shocked. If there was anything worse that could have happened, I wanted that to happen at that very moment. I was standing near the cake, at the very same place where I once overheard my melody queen singing happy birthday for Ruchi. I could smell her. I turned around to look for her. She was not there. She was nothing more than a figment of my imagination. An illusion, which left me the moment I needed it the most. Her memory transformed everything in front of my eyes. My mind was nothing more than a blank sheet of paper waiting for her to come and fill it with her words.

'You don't look good when serious.' Ruchi was back, a little bit saner this time. It seemed her intoxication was thrown out of her body with her exuberant dance moves.

'As if I ever look good.' I said, trying to seek sympathy.

'Wait a minute! You're done with your braces, wow. You've got such a cute smile.' Ruchi exclaimed. I blushed, but the shyness didn't stay for long, it was soon overpowered with grief.

I didn't say a thing. Neither did she. A random couple came to greet her and once again, I was stranded in an eerie desolation amongst so many people. I was playing around with the birthday knife. I took it in my hand and tried to cut my wrist with it, with no success. Alas, it was a plastic one. I had this funny urge of slitting my throat with it. An abrupt smile erupted on my face thereafter, which was suppressed as abruptly it appeared.

'If you really want to cut your wrist, try this.' Ruchi said, handing over a sharp knife to me. I smiled back, didn't say a word. She was holding a glass of rum in her hand. She offered it to me, which I politely declined.

'She called me today. She said she wouldn't be able to come to the party. She seemed very unhappy. She asked me not to ask her the reason. I didn't ask her anything. She came over to my place just to give me my gift, didn't speak a word though. She looked terribly shattered.'

I choked on hearing her last two words. It was me. Not anyone else, but me. She was still angry with me. But how would I patch up when she is not ready to listen to me? All my plans of kneeling down, gifting her my book and thereafter proposing to her in front of everyone (yes, that too was in the list, I kept it as a surprise!) seemed to have turned into ashes.

'Did she have a fight with her mother once again?' Ruchi asked.

'No. I mean I don't know.' I lied.

'Wait, which reminds me that she had given me a letter to give to you. Let me fetch it.' I was clueless. While she went towards her pile of birthday gifts to fetch the letter from the bag, it killed every little piece of hope that I had in me.

'God only knows how I could resist opening and reading it. I was so damn curious to know what had happened to her.' Ruchi muttered as she came back. I was more interested in snatching what was in her hand and reading it. I tried to grab it. Ruchi didn't allow.

'I want to read it too.' She said curtly.

'It's personal, come on!'

'It's my birthday, you can't deny my wish. Come on!' She mimicked me; her drunken state seemed to have seized her consciousness.

'I've a better gift for you. I'll give that to you only when you leave me alone with it.' I said, irritably.

'Ok.' She agreed. I was already dying to read what the letter said and if Ruchi had not agreed that time, her birthday would have been spoilt since either I would have pushed her away or I would have thrown her on the giant cake.

I pulled out the book from the bag, carefully seeing that it was meant to be gifted to Ruchi. It was wrapped in a newspaper.

'Oh, another book! That too wrapped in newspaper. What is it, a second hand elementary trigonomotery book?'

'It's not just another book. It's a special book. Unwrap it.' I said, unexcited, despite the thrill on her face. I was anxious to read what was in the letter. I slowly moved out of the scene to read what the letter had to say to me.

There was a huge commotion inside the restaurant. I realized that my book would have stolen the show. However, I was putting my heart and soul at a bigger objective i.e. opening the envelope without tearing it, standing under the street-light. When it came to Tanya and things about Tanya, I always tried being classy. I had to complement her after all. Now, thinking about my last action, I admit that I was being a jerk.

At last when I failed to achieve anything by being orderly, I twisted my head around. Seeing no Tanya, I just tore the envelope apart and threw it on the ground. I opened the letter. I lay back on the street-light pole. It was hand-written, in a handwriting that was immaculate and artistic. There was no 'Dear Kanav/Bubu/Love' embellishing the beginning. It was serious. It turned much more serious with every line that I read.

It's not about you or me or us. It's not about the fact that we dated or we had been in love. It's about respect. In the last 24 hours, no matter how hard I tried to convince myself, your harsh words echoed in my ears and made me tremble every single time. I feel emotionally raped. You've been consistently saying that it was a silly reason why I got frenzied, but as a woman, and as a lover, I feel shattered. Disrespect is worse than betrayal, Kanav. It breaks the very essence of a relationship.

Maybe you didn't mean what you said; maybe you wanted to say something else and accidentally showed the dark side of yours. But what if you meant everything you said, when you said that I was no more than an average loser stuck in your life from nowhere, when you said that I was the biggest mistake of your life, when you dared to not only abuse me but went on to my mother. You couldn't have said that if you didn't mean it, no matter how angry you would have been. It hurts, Kanav. It hurts a lot. I've never felt this bad, since there always had been the faith that somebody loved me more than I ever desired, that kept me going but last day, you even took that faith away from me and now I'm nothing more than a woman wasted in love.

I couldn't believe my ears when I heard you last time. I thought it couldn't be you. It couldn't be my Kanav. I thought so because I cared. But, you didn't. You went on; until you made sure that you shredded every bit of love from within me. Maybe I don't mean anything to you. Or maybe I do. I don't know. And the truth is, I don't want to know anymore. I've lost everything I had. I always wished my love to be utopian, uncontaminated with any such ill events. But this has taken away my power even to wish. How could I ever be convinced that you didn't mean what you said? Your words *won't convince me, since your words can't stand strong against your own words.*

You need to fight with yourself first. I don't think it's the right time for us to be together because where there's lack of respect; there'll be lack of love. I'll be gone in a day and I would give you ample space to introspect, come face to face with yourself, realize whether it is love or anything else that is holding you on to me, for love is build on respect. Learn to respect. And before that, respect respect.

I'll not wait for you. I might move on with my life and would love if you do the same. I'll be happy. I have all the more reasons to be happy since now I'll no more be guilty of lying to my mother. Kanav, it's my humble request to you that if you actually love me, please do not ever try to reach me. Let's stand this test of sacrifice; if we're destined to be together, nothing could stop us.

I loved you. Take care.

Tanya

I slid down the pole, having nothing left to say, think or see. I was blankly staring at the wheels of the cars parked in front of me; my palm had unconsciously crushed the letter. My feet seemed to have turned to stone. The commotion inside the room spread outside as I heard the shout, 'Hey, here's the author.' I could see a familiar crowd surrounding me. Ruchi ran through the crowd, bisecting the two gayish gentlemen in front and rushed to me, screaming, 'What happened to you? Are you okay?'

I was a dead man. My body never felt so heavy as much as it did then. It was not until the same two gentlemen offered their shoulders that I could get up. The crushed letter fell on the ground, which Ruchi picked up and skimmed through, without my permission. I didn't mind. I was clueless as to what had happened to mind what was happening. The gentlemen took proper care of me and dropped me on the sofa inside 'Waikiki'. Two girls came forward to me, looking thoroughly interested in having a conversation. After I remained as unconcerned as the sofa I was sitting on, one of them said, 'Hey, you're amazing. I just went through a couple of paragraphs of the beginning. You write so well.'

I mumbled an indistinct thanks to them. 'Can I have your phone number?' One of them said. It was the first time a girl was asking for my number, it was the first time the ball was in my court and it was the first time I wasn't interested at all.

'I don't use a cellphone anymore.' I said. They made weird faces, whispered to each other and went away in a huff.

Ruchi followed and meekly sat besides me, put her head on my shoulders and patted my back. She mumbled an almost mute 'I'm sorry' to me and handed over the letter. I ignored it. She couldn't do anything about it. I was the one who was responsible for the mess. Unable to take on the awkwardness, she went forward to cut the cake. She didn't ask me to come along, for which I'm immensely grateful. The sofa was doing good to my completely immobile self.

I was still in a trance. I looked around. Some people were looking at me. I could hear indistinct happy birthday songs coming from near the centre, people putting the cream on their girlfriends as make-up and darkness, silence and nothingness pervading everything that I could see. I slept.

When woken up, I hurriedly finished my dinner, without saying a word and sneaked out of what used to be my favourite restaurant, taking a bottle of vodka in my bag. One of the gayish gentleman agreed to drop me back to my hostel, for he was too overwhelmed riding with an author.

I sat next to him, gulped two to three neat shots of vodka and tried to remain sane. It was difficult. I shredded her letter into pieces and put it into my pocket. The gentleman didn't say a word. He tried sparking off a conversation with me, but I didn't respond. I was too preoccupied in myself. I hurled my book that was to be gifted to Tanya at the stray dogs. 'If not the bitch, let it be dogs who read it,' I uttered in disgust.

'Hey Kanav, you've written a love story. Come on, tell me, what do you think of love?' He tried to be genuinely nice.

'Fuck respect. Fuck love. And fuck every bitch. Life will fuck you otherwise.' I screamed and dropped off to sleep. When I woke up, I was in my hostel room. The first thing that I checked when I woke up that day was my pants, and I was glad to realize that it was right there, but the belt was missing. I don't know how I landed up in my hostel room the very next day. Whether the gentleman carried me in his arms to my room, or was it any of my friends assisted him is something that I do not know, to this date.

Epilogue

Your life sucks when you have nothing to look forward to every morning. For some, notifications and likes on their status messages were enough. But not for me. I wasn't the kind of guy who could take life as it came. I was in love. So much that I could do anything for her, even stop talking to her. I made an inward promise to myself of never ever trying to contact her until she reached back to me.

Her letter had been engraved on my soul; every action of mine seemed to run through a scan of what she expected me to be. I was following the path she laid out for me. The path of betterment, perhaps. By being away, she made me struggle but at the same time, evolved the human side of me.

The next month, I started writing more avidly, this time trying my hand at short stories and was glad to realize that I was good at it. Writing came up as my newly-found companion, helping me to distract my attention from what could have otherwise seemed like a depressing never-ending wait and longing.

My book struck a chord with the readers; people could relate themselves to my story. Many people started taking it as an inspirational read for those who were not good-looking, who had braces and aspired to get a beautiful girlfriend. Suddenly, I was being treated like a love guru, with mails like...

'My girlfriend ditched me for my classmate. How should I win her back?'

I always wanted to reply to them, but considering my own limitation as a person, I could just relate from my own experience the one big learning in love : 'If you want to be in love, don't ever be an asshole.' I had been an asshole once and had been left alone for over a month now, with no signs of mercy coming my way.

A month after the book were published, my Dad read it and laughingly, said to me, 'I liked your novel. I would have liked it more had you been thirty and written it.' I was glad that he was such a sport.

My mother read my book and loved it. I was shocked when she especially called me and related how engrossed she had become while reading that she forgot to switch off the gas-stove and the entire bowl of milk was evaporated. And very recently, to my embarrassment, she has recommended it to all of her friends. I just hope that they keep mum so as to keep my Mum happy. Also, she's done with the passport and she is eager to accompany me. Now, I've no problems to that too. Maybe after this book, she changes her plans.

My trio of friends is awesome, as always. They've specifically asked me to dedicate a chapter to each one of them in my next book. Aryan is delighted to notice that my readers are crazy about him. He answers all the fan-mails that mention him. He has been getting more friend requests than me.

Anuj, with much more experience in the domain of complicated relationships, together with our gabby philoshopher Sameer have taken over the task of replying to my fan-mails. Anuj says that it makes him feel worthy of contributing to the higher good of society, while Sameer says it makes him rehearse for his future ambition of becoming a self-help guru. God save my readers, who ask for advice on love!

Last but not the least, coming to Tanya, there has been no news from her side. A day after the birthday party, I found out that she had blocked me from facebook, deleted her email account and severed every existing mode of communication from her. Interestingly, it didn't make me unhappy. For all I know, I have been religiously following what she had asked me to. I can sacrifice her for her sake. I don't know whether things would be great in future (read: the third book) or whether things would remain as dry as they are now. But, the good thing is I'm hopeful. And when there's hope, there's happiness.

I still shiver in awkward fear upon thinking about my lost belt. I have never touched Vodka thereafter. No wonder, Ouch! That 'hearts'.

A story should never end, it should always begin. So, here I begin…

From the next book, the last one in the Kanav- Tanya trilogy…

Meet the Queen of Venice…

It had been two months since my novel was published. The response had been stunning, much more than what I had expected. Every day over a dozen mails from readers all around India would be occupying my inbox. Some contained heart-warming praises, some contained genuine criticisms, which were in good spirit to help me improve as an author. Some were cynical, which I read and hardly cared to reply.

The sudden spurt of fame seemed wonderful, being one of the rarest feelings I've ever encountered. I was at my life's most enchanting period - the period of utmost creative joy. It was during that time that this girl with the name 'queenofvenice' read my entire work and decided to throw some brickbats in the comments section of the promotional blog for my novel. But unlike others, she had a different take on it - completely different.

'Your work was like-able but I hated you totally. If there was the word slut for a man, you would be that. I wonder how people could give you so much attention.' She wrote.

I was thoroughly entertained and a little bit confused. I liked being called a 'man-slut'. It was the rarest of compliments that one could have ever received in life. Not that I loved it for the very feel of it but it actually gave me a better opinion of myself, as far as women were concerned. That was so because my experience in this field was painfully limited.

Did she confuse me with any of the characters, or has my presence as a writer been so insipid? I showed it to Anuj, who got outraged and started typing rubbish, when I stopped and asked him to let me reply.

I began, 'Thank you. It was a pleasure getting attention from you. I didn't know that I could ever be complimented for such a cause. Thanks again.'

Within an hour, she posted another comment, 'I was not giving you attention! I was just letting you know what your status is.'

'I can't understand the reason behind the immense hatred in you. If it's my novel that's the reason, let me remind you that everything there is fictitious.' I immediately replied.

'And I would not like being called a slut in public, so shoot each of your anger-shots at me at the given id – kanav.bajaj@gmail.com.' I turned flirtatious. Her audacity being the reason for my audacity.

A moment later, *queenofvenice@gmail.com* sent me an add request. As always, carrying on with my earlier wimpish self when it came to strangers, I couldn't dare to start the chat. She took the initiative.

queenofvenice: *It's 2 o' clock at night. I'm not too fond of talking to guys at night, and more so your kind - tchtch.*

I: Neither am I. I never talk to guys, especially at this time.

'Thank God, for giving me a sense of humour.' I thought.

queenofvenice: You asshole! What do you think you are?

I felt insulted. I wanted to block her then and forever. But I was new to attention and I liked it. However, my self-respect asked my timid self to rebel. I could not tolerate the bullshit.

I: Wait a minute. Who the fuck are you?

I was suspicious that this would be a gag that one of my hostel-friends would be playing with me, at the middle of the night.

queenofvenice: I'm a hardcore feminist. And I'm against every person who considers woman as a sex-object.

The doubt that the Queen of Venice might be residing in my hostel almost faded. My worldly hostel-friends would never have tried to act as feminists in their entire life, not even for the sake of a gag, leave alone being a hardcore one. I tried to search her id on social networking websites, and ultimately I could find her on Facebook. Her name was Shambhavi and she seemed to be pretty. Another reason to talk. I read the conversation once again.

I: Wait a minute. Where have I talked about women as sex-objects in my novel?

queenofvenice: You have not but your feelings were visible all throughout your piece of shit.

I (sarcastically): Oh really, then what made you lick that piece of shit in its entirety?

queenofvenice: You wrote it well. Engrossing, but full of shit.

I: So, you like shit?

queenofvenice: *I hate asses, like you!*

Curious!

I: Who are you? I mean where are you from? What do you do?

queenofvenice: *I'm Shambhavi, from XYZ university. I kick asses of asses.*

I: That's a good way to contribute to the society. BTW, nice name.

I was flirting with a complete stranger for the second time in my life. The first time was when I was seven, when I received a tight slap on my cheek in reciprocation which eventually made me a wimp.

queenofvenice: *Indeed. So, how many people have you slept with?*

Shocker! Totally unexpected question! I got a little frenzied.

I: Is it a part of your hardcore feminist survey?

queenofvenice: *No, it isn't. Answer me.*

I thought of playing a gimmick.

I: Ummm...one...two....three...four-five...umm....in total 24.

queenofvenice: *Bloody slut! I knew you would be so. When did you lose it?*

I (trying to act innocent): What are you talking about?

queenofvenice: *Your stupid mind, you sucker.*

Pretty brash, I must say. But pretty different. Plus, two pretty eyes were icing on the cake. How could I not take her abuses? A moment of flirtation, a quantum leap of satisfaction.

It took me a while to think of the most imperfect age to lose 'it'.

I: I lost that, when I was...17.

queenofvenice: *To whom?*

I: To JEE! :P

queenofvenice: *Asshole. Would you like to meet me?*

Now that was weird. Firstly, she hates me. Secondly, she abuses me. Thirdly, she wants to meet me. I was dead nervous. She seemed to be one of 'those' kinds, if you get 'bonded' to what I mean.

I: Not now. I'm sleepy.

queenofvenice: *Tomorrow?*

I: But why? I mean why do you want to meet me? You hate me. You are a hardcore feminist and as you've realized, I am a misogynist. And lastly, you think that I'm a slut.

queenofvenice: *That's why.*

I: You're acting like one.

queenofvenice: *I'm not. I'm not acting.*

I read the last line twice. My jaws fell down and my eyes were transfixed to the computer screen. I was shivering. I couldn't reply.

queenofvenice: *Check out my pictures.* [hyperlink]

I clicked on the hyperlink. Her pictures opened. Seeing them, my mind was completely blown. I'd never seen anything like that ever before. They were ...

Coming soon...